The Society of Scrooge

1845

The Further Trials and Triumphs of

Scrooge and His Companions

by

Judy La Salle

A sequel to *Scrooge, the Year After*

Acknowledgments

Many thanks to my husband Rod for his positive support in so many loving ways, including taking the time to discuss things, and do research. He is also a lifesaver when it comes to creativity with computers and formatting. My sister, Nancy, kept me constantly in her prayers and always gave me loving encouragement. She was willing to discuss ideas, read drafts and give me honest feedback. My friend, Lynne, spent many hours reading and re-reading the initial draft, giving suggestions, making corrections, and urging me on.

Martin Sach at the London Canal Museum was extremely patient and helpful in sharing information about the English canal system in the 19th Century, and he always responded promptly to my questions. Taryk Welburn, Search Engine Assistant with the National Railway Museum in York, England, was very helpful in putting me on the right routes, helping me find stations that Scrooge may have used, and in answering my general questions about railway travel in 1845.

Our fifteen-pound cat, Baby, was also on hand whenever I sat down to write. I could rely on him to stretch out over whatever I was working on, particularly the keyboard as I tried to type.

THE SOCIETY OF
SCROOGE

CHAPTER ONE

The Salon

Scrooge was very uncomfortable and was made more so by his attempts to appear at ease. Never in his life had he encountered such outlandish persons. Much of what they said and did was so ungoverned by common civilized constraints that he was hard put to know how to respond. For that reason, instead of attempting general conversation with them, he politely observed their peculiarities. Truth be told, he must admit that they were, on the whole, quite fascinating.

"Have some more tea, Mister Scrooge?" It was Mrs. Sotherton who addressed him.

"I will, thank you. It's very good and just what I needed this afternoon." Scrooge and Mrs. Sotherton had only recently become acquainted, but he felt as if he had known her for decades, having long been aware of her formidable and powerful reputation. She was also the mother of his particular friend, Mrs. Rebecca Langstone, who was

1

a very lovely widow for whom he had an unexpected and growing fondness.

Scrooge could still feel somewhat out-of-place in social settings, although no one would have been aware of his unease. It had been well over a twelvemonth since his character was renewed by that persistent parade of spirits, but what others took to be an overnight miracle of transformation, Scrooge was experiencing over time, and it had not all been pleasant. It was true that his personality and character were being re-formed, but it was much like a stone taking shape under a sculptor's tools, and he had felt every blow of the chisel. On occasion, it could be excruciating.

Mrs. Sotherton knew or, at the very least, suspected that her daughter was fond of Scrooge and she admitted to herself that she could see how that might be. Mr. Scrooge was an attractive man in his fifties and was a lively conversationalist with a penchant for becoming embroiled in adventure. She knew as much from her daughter's account of his discoveries regarding the untimely death of his sister, Fan. Fan had died twenty-five years earlier, which made his discoveries regarding her death all the more an accomplishment. After some prodding, he had even related some of the particulars of those events to Mrs. Sotherton herself, which only increased her admiration and endeared him to her all the more. At the close of their first conversation over tea in Rebecca's home, she had become convinced of her own desire to maintain contact with, and enjoy the company of, this very unique gentleman.

As Mrs. Sotherton contemplated his addition to her afternoon salon, Mr. Scrooge leaned in. With a subtle tilt of his head toward a bearded man, he asked, "And who is the unblinking fellow who is set on staring at you? He is sitting in front of the one who is juggling your silver spoons." He might have asked instead, "Who is the bearded fellow sitting not ten feet from the woman who is walking in circles, reading poetry aloud to no one but herself?"

With a slight tilt of her head, Mrs. Sotherton smiled and spoke in a low voice. "That, my dear man, is Mr. Durand. He is an eccentric gentleman of Continental persuasion, and he likes to pretend to himself, and to others, that I was his inamorata in a previous life. I haven't the heart, nor the ability, to dissuade him in his delusions. He occasionally likes to remind me of a moonlit terrace we shared in some exotic place, or a famous personage (long dead, of course) with whom he believes we shared acquaintance. I admit I can be thoroughly entertained by his illusions and he is never rude or impudent, so I find his company easy to endure, at least in the short term, and only on occasion."

Scrooge could not imagine tolerating such an irrational character until he recalled his own penchant for communing with the dead. He was thinking of Marley, of course, with whom he continued to have occasional and irregular social intercourse. He had no way of knowing whether the encounters with his long-dead friend were real, imagined, or even providential, but he couldn't help wondering if Mrs. Sotherton would be as accepting of his invisible companion as she was those personages hovering about Mr. Durand's head. *Would she simply dismiss me as thoroughly mad and conclude that I am not such desirable company, after all, for her or her daughter?*

As if reading his mind, Mrs. Sotherton remarked, "I see in your expression, Sir, that this gathering may be a little too much for you to take in, particularly at one sitting. Not only are some of my guests a bit odd, but the eccentricities of each, when taken together, can be somewhat overwhelming." Then she smiled as if to reassure him, and added, "I realize it is selfish on my part to explain this to you, but I would not have you think ill of me simply because I enjoy an occasional foray into the ridiculous." She continued to explain.

"I don't often invite the 'outlandish' to my salons, but there are those times when I find I simply need an afternoon of total diversion." She sighed and touched his sleeve very lightly as she said, "I apologize if I invited you to the wrong gathering for your first introduction to my hospitality, but I knew, from Rebecca, that the unknown does not frighten you. So, you see, at the time I issued you my invitation I believed you would not only manage very well with these temperaments, but that you might even gain a bit of enjoyment. I still hope so, even though your expression belies it." He noticed she was smiling.

Scrooge was about to reply that he was up to any challenge she might offer, but as he placed his cup and saucer on the nearby side table, a woman approached and addressed Mrs. Sotherton. Waving an elegant hand toward Scrooge, she announced to her hostess, "My dear friend, you presented Mr. Scrooge to me earlier, but I find I need to know more about him, other than his name and his position. Will you give me additional details, or shall I pry them from him myself?" Her voice cascaded into the room like warm oil, and it was anything but a whisper. In fact, she easily commanded the attention of others, even those to whom she was not speaking. That was evidenced by the heads turning in their direction, and Scrooge attempted to hide his face behind one of his hands in a seemingly relaxed pose.

Although he was taken aback by her boldness, Scrooge was also captured by her self-confidence and, as would most men in his position, her appearance. She was entirely lovely, and she possessed an air of self-assurance and humor that was almost masculine, yet somehow appealing. He knew from their earlier introduction that this was none other than Emma Aldrich, an actress currently appearing at the Adelphi Theatre. He was also well aware that he was, at that moment, her captive audience because of the undivided attention he was honor-bound to give her. Due to her easy, yet demanding and enchanting performance, Scrooge suspected that Emma Aldrich was always on stage.

Mrs. Sotherton rose and offered her chair to Miss Aldrich, making the excuse that she should see to her other guests, and the actress gracefully took the seat. Looking directly into Scrooge's eyes, she asked, "Have you a wife?" She began a slow, suggestive smile as she quickly added, "Not that I ever concern myself with such details, you understand. I find that wives can be a necessary evil, but men generally seek their amusements elsewhere, do they not?"

Scrooge leaned back to create distance between them and tried to reply, but even a simple "No" refused to come out. He had never encountered such a bold female and was not yet equipped to deal with such aggressive and improper behavior. He would need several moments in which to compose a cogent sentence, but he hadn't the time. He was the mouse, cornered by the cat, and there was no mistaking that she planned to toy with him. *Where on earth is Mrs. Sotherton, confound the woman. In fact, confound both of these free-thinking women!*

As if on cue, Mrs. Sotherton reappeared with the entreaty that the Dimpley twins were in desperate need of hearing Miss Aldrich recite some lines from her current play. Ever the performer, the actress excused herself and rose to be led away to awaiting adoration. Taking advantage of the situation, Scrooge stood quickly and set his course for the door, determined to escape. He knew it was rude to leave without saying goodbye, but a sensible person could tolerate only so much nonsense. He liked and appreciated Mrs. Sotherton very much and would definitely continue to count her among his favored acquaintances, but he was doubtful that he would again subject himself to so much nonsense in exchange for a good cup of tea. He would send a note of thanks rather than risk being detained, or, worse, being re-captured by this band of extraordinary persons. As he reached the door he was sorely tempted to turn back around and deliver a loud "Humbug!" to the lot of them.

Once outside, Scrooge could breathe more easily, so he forced his neck and back muscles to relax by shrugging his shoulders several times. It was late afternoon and he was in need of more appropriate company which, naturally, turned his thoughts to Mrs. Langstone.

Scrooge wanted to see her, and even though it would mean he would arrive unannounced, he knew that would be acceptable. He and she were both of an age where they were not bound by every societal constraint. No, they would not thumb their noses at convention entirely, but nor did they allow it to force them into meaningless rituals. They had even agreed to use each other's given names, at least when they met privately.

Scrooge admired Rebecca Langstone a great deal. She was a widow of middle age and very attractive, in both appearance and character. In fact, she had stood by him and assisted in his most recent adventure of uncovering the cause of his sister Fan's death so many years earlier. Mrs. Langstone was his friend and willing partner in his endeavors and he would even go so far as to allow that she was a possible soulmate, or perhaps more. He had not admitted as much to anyone, but he had vague desires where she was concerned, and he was fairly certain she was aware of them. Since she had not spurned his small hints of endearment, he dared hope she returned the sentiment. Still, he would not hope for too much since he had not yet forgotten how she deftly avoided the mistletoe kissing ball on Christmas Eve.

It wasn't that long ago that Scrooge would not have considered taking a cab because it would mean handing over a few shillings to a complete stranger who may or may not know how to handle a horse. However, since he was no longer an unpleasant pinch-penny, he quickly hailed the first one he saw, eager to remove himself further from the hubbub he had narrowly escaped. Climbing in, he directed the cabby to Mrs. Langstone's home in Russell Square.

⊂Зൟ⊃

"Ebenezer," Mrs. Langstone said with delight, upon receiving Scrooge. "How nice it is to see you. Is something afoot, or have you simply come to wish me a good afternoon? Either would be welcome, you know." Soon they were seated in her morning room, which was her personal space and not used for general callers. He was grateful for every moment they had spent in this room and he appreciated the privilege of being entertained less formally by his hostess. Before long, Mrs. Langstone recalled something, and asked, "Were you not to attend one of my mother's salons today? Did you do so?"

Blast! I should have known she would recall that invitation, and for the second time today I'm unprepared with an answer that will not offend. "I did," replied Scrooge simply. How much should he relate regarding his impressions of Mrs. Sotherton's guests, since Rebecca might think them a censorious assessment of her mother. He was saved from the decision when she noticed his expression.

"Ebenezer, your face is flushed, and you seem at a loss for words." With a slight smile she tilted her head to one side and said, "Let me guess. You were privy to one of Mother's gatherings of the odd, the silly and the preposterous. Those assemblies are always a bit awkward for the uninitiated, but she enjoys an occasional foray into the ridiculous and sometimes uses those gatherings to assess new friends. Did you pass the examination?" She was confident that he had.

Scrooge was abashed, but there was nothing for it but honesty, so he told the God's truth. "Rebecca, I failed to measure up. I was totally overwhelmed by her guests and I suspect that not only will she never invite me to her home in future, I have even ruined any prospect of a decent acquaintance!" He shifted in his seat and leaned forward. As if someone might overhear, he lowered his voice before admitting, "I have never been among so many extraordinary people in my life, and I was unable to act with any amount of civility. In fact, I actually sneaked out when no one was looking, and I did not even extend a polite, 'Thank you, and good-bye.'" He was clearly mortified and exposed his greatest fear by quickly adding, "Please tell me this will not undo all that you and I have shared over the past few months. I hope very much to remain your friend, even if your mother publicly disavows me before the whole of England!"

Mrs. Langstone looked at him for several seconds before she reacted and, of a sudden, her expression changed to mirth. Her smile became a giggle, then she was overcome by a hearty laugh. Scrooge had never heard her laugh so hard in all of their times together. Just as he was on the verge of offense, she managed to calm herself. She wiped her eyes with her handkerchief, shook her head and said, "Oh, my dear friend, you have given me the most enjoyment I've had in weeks, and you will be surprised to know that I am certain you not only passed my mother's muster, you did so with flags flying! She loves an ending she could not predict, and your devious departure was no doubt enough to convince her that you are quite the diversion. Not many would have had the courage to act so independently and chance her disapproval. She now knows that you are not afraid of her, and she craves that because she grows weary of so many sycophants and flatterers.

As she put away her handkerchief, Mrs. Langstone continued. "To address your concerns, our friendship is not in danger. How could it be? We have shared so many good and bad times in only a few months that I admit I look forward to whatever our acquaintance brings in future. Your exposure to today's tomfoolery, and your reaction to it, only confirm that wherever you go there will be the unexpected; the difficult, perhaps; and the enjoyable. I would not, for anything, forfeit that. Now, do please stay to share my simple, cold supper and we can converse of other things."

Scrooge eagerly accepted the invitation, but noticed Mrs. Langstone had cleverly avoided saying she cared for him, mentioning only the entertainment she garnered from his acquaintance. She had also deftly guided the conversation away from the subject of their friendship. Perhaps she was being as careful as he about declaring herself to any degree. It was, after all, up to the gentleman to declare himself first, and he was far too unsure of anything at this time. There was much to gain in their association, but there was also much to lose, should either of them misstep, and neither wanted to be the one to do so.

CHAPTER TWO

Edwin Carter

The following morning Scrooge was eager to be in his counting house. He had thoroughly enjoyed the previous evening with Mrs. Langstone but was still reeling a bit from his time with what he had come to think of as "Mrs. Sotherton's Circus." His intent was not condemnation, it was simply that the term aptly fit his estimation of the gathering. However, just as he was about to step over the worn and welcoming threshold of the counting-house, Scrooge was struck with a terrible possibility. It flew in the face of all Mrs. Langstone had said in order to reassure him, but what if — Dear Lord — what if he had been invited to "The Circus" because he was, himself, an oddity! He quickly shook his head as if to dislodge such a thought from his mind. It would not do to entertain such ideas.

So, with yesterday's scenes still toying with his brain, Scrooge found it reassuring to be back in familiar surroundings populated by men of sound mind and sensible behavior. He was fond of them all, from his dear nephew and partner Fred to his chief clerk Bob Cratchit and Cratchit's handsome Welsh assistant, Homer Probert. There was also young Peter Cratchit, who occasionally played the office dog's body, and was a very big help, at that. They all got on well together, and it pleased him. The Scrooge of two years ago would have taken no notice of whether anyone got along or not, nor given a fig if they hadn't. He would merely have demanded that they cease their jabbering and mind their work, if they valued their positions!

Contrary to his old habits of snarling and snapping at anyone with whom he came into contact, these days Scrooge enjoyed conversing with the businessmen who stopped in to affect a transaction, as well as the occasional visitor, including Scrooge's old friend Dick Wilkins. Scrooge also loved the office building, itself. There was the scent of the place, with its dark aged wood, the many stacks of balance books, and its coal-driven warmth. The good-natured bustle provided a fine living for everyone and earned a pretty profit for him, and Fred. Mostly, it furnished friendship and the sort of camaraderie his new nature required. Yes, it was a good, solid establishment and there was not one actress, juggler, nor communicant with the unseen among them – other than himself, of course.

Not long after their morning greetings had been completed and all had settled to their tasks for the day, the door was flung wide open, straining its old hinges, and an oversized, well-dressed gentleman plunged through like a battering ram. He was smiling as if his nature expected the same in return, and he moved quickly, but purposefully.

He was obviously used to getting things done and would waste no time in doing them. He removed his hat before speaking.

"Gentlemen!", he announced, his voice booming through the halls like the retort of a field cannon. "I see from the shingle outside that this is the establishment of Scrooge and Symons, which I believe I once knew as Scrooge and Marley. If so, you may welcome me back, for I am returned from America, where I have garnered property and fortune, and I am ready to conduct more business!" With that, he laughed a hearty contagious laugh and was instantly recognized by both Scrooge and Cratchit.

"Edwin Carter!", they cried in unison. No one could ever forget the only man in the British Empire to actually convince Scrooge's old partner, and fellow miser, to stake him his fare to America. Carter had been an abject failure at every endeavor he undertook in England, yet, for some mysterious reason, Marley personally staked him in his overseas venture. No one believed it of Marley then, and it was near impossible to believe the transformation of the successful personage standing before them. Scrooge must tell Marley of the man's success the next time Marley floated through Scrooge's bedchamber wall.

Looking around, Mr. Carter asked, "Is my old benefactor no longer here then? I surely hope he hasn't gone far, for I have money to repay and I very much want to shake his hand and share my adventures over a pint." His smile wilted as he noticed how still the company had become, and he rightly discerned that each was waiting for the other to speak. It naturally fell to Scrooge to explain.

"I, um, regret to say that my old partner, Jacob Marley, has been dead these past eight years, although I can assure you that wherever he is I am certain he will know of the benefit of his loan. *I'll see to that, and I plan to wring a few more details out of him while I'm at it!* As you may recall, he was never a man to part with his money, nor was I, but for some reason he did not fully explain, he became convinced that he was divinely ordered to purchase your passage, as well as stake you in your venture. I couldn't believe it of him, nor could Cratchit here, and I tried to dissuade him, but he would not be budged."

"Divinely ordered, eh?" Slapping his thigh with his hat, Carter cried, "Yes! He believed he was." Mr. Carter then removed his coat, which Cratchit hung on the coat rack, took a nearby chair, and continued, correctly assuming that the company would find his tale to be of interest.

"I was shaking in my shoes the morning I asked Mr. Marley for the loan, but I had been turned away by everyone else and he was my last hope. If he were to say 'no,' I had already chosen the bridge from which I would take a fatal leap. You see, I had nothing left, and even though I suspected from his reputation that he would prefer my jumping to my death than that he part with a ha'penny, he surprised me. I had nothing to lose but my life which, at that point, seemed worth little, so I chanced being rejected, and ended up right here, in this very building."

With the unfocused stare of one recalling the past, Mr. Carter paused, and no one dared move. Cratchit did, however, slowly nod his head when Mr. Carter looked his way and said, "Mr. Cratchit, you may recall escorting me to Mr. Marley's office, where I stood quaking before his desk as he ignored me and continued to scribble on some paper. You returned to your station and at some point, which seemed an eternity to me, he looked up and snarled, 'Well, what is it you want?'

"In that instant I near turned and ran, but since this truly was a matter of life or death to me, I rattled off my request and steeled myself for the disappointment that was to follow, not to mention my upcoming demise at that bridge. Instead, Mr. Marley sat stock still and turned as white as a ghost, as if he had actually seen one. It was so real that I near turned 'round to see what might be lurking behind me! Neither of us spoke for some time; he just sitting there and I still standing, until he said simply, 'You may have your loan – at ten percent interest.'" At that moment Homer accidentally knocked his quill from his writing desk, and in the hush it resounded like the drop of a rail spike. He quickly retrieved it, and Mr. Carter continued.

"Once settled in New York, I sent Mr. Marley a letter giving him my direction and informing him that I planned to make good the loan. I received a letter from him some months later. I'll never forget its contents because it explained his astounding reaction to my request, as well as his reason for granting it.

"It all came down to the fact that the night before I made my appeal, Mr. Marley dreamed, or had a vision, that an unlikely ne'er-do-well was going to ask him for the exact amount I named, in order to leave England. In that dream he was instructed by an apparition to loan me the money from his own fortune, rather than funds from this establishment. He was told that, depending upon whether or not he complied, the outcome would be, for him, I believe he said, 'a matter of mercy, or judgment.' When I stood before him that morning and brought his dream to life in such detail, he was so taken aback that he did as he had been told. I've often wondered why he corresponded with me and laid out all of the particulars, but now I suppose we're never to know."

Everyone sat in stunned silence while Scrooge thought to himself, *Marley, you and I have much to discuss! So, you were visited by a spirit, too . . . and in the same bedchamber I now occupy.*

"Well, my new friends," said Mr. Carter as he stood to take his leave. "I have taken enough of your time this morning, but there is a particular investment I wish to explore, and I want it done through this office. It will be a substantial transaction, so, when may I call again, to test the idea?" After some discussion it was agreed that he would return in two days. Meanwhile, there were other contracts to complete, meetings to attend and records to keep, which sent everyone back to work.

CR&O

In two days' time Mr. Carter reappeared. He was eager to begin his new endeavors and was honest in admitting that his need to do so was somewhat based on his desire to make a successful name for himself in England. He had left the shores of his beloved country as a total failure and was now returned with pounds enough to become even richer, should he invest wisely. It was reasonable that he should want that success to benefit the office that had made it possible for him to travel to America in the first place.

Mr. Carter was disappointed to be unable to once again speak with Marley, so he made arrangements to repay the business itself, since Scrooge was unwilling to receive the funds into his own personal accounts. Mr. Carter would not hear of anything else because, as he insisted, "I am a fair man and it would be wrong to dismiss a debt simply because the benefactor has died." He further explained his reasoning by adding, "From what I understand, Mr. Scrooge, you are, for all intents and purposes, Mr. Marley's beneficiary. So, that settles it." It was the beginning of a very satisfactory relationship between Mr. Carter and the office of Scrooge and Symons. Through the transfers of money it was also verified that Mr. Carter was indeed rich, but he was not frivolous. He was as prudent a businessman as Scrooge, and as honest. He was also very generous when he saw a need. He fit in nicely, both as an investor and as a friend.

The venture proposed by Mr. Carter concerned employing the use of steam, as opposed to wind power, in the Netherlands, and possibly Belgium or Denmark. It also required that someone make a preliminary trip to at least one or two of those countries. It was decided that Fred would go since he had previous experience working with Dutch traders. Even though Scrooge was naturally more adept overall, it was his desire that Fred expand his knowledge. Mr. Carter would accompany whoever made the latter trips, to actually put the plan into action, but that would not come about until some basic agreements had been contracted. Meanwhile, prior to Fred's departure, arrangements would be made; dispatches sent and received; meetings and accommodations confirmed, and any necessary money made available.

CHAPTER THREE

Miss Emma Aldrich

Mrs. Dilber had been Scrooge's housekeeper for some years now and had proven herself to be loyal, trustworthy and efficient. It wasn't so, however, until Scrooge became a better man and, therefore, a better employer. In earlier times she was what could only be described as a slattern, whose concern was for the few coins she could cheat out of Scrooge, rather than what she could do to actually earn them. They were, in fact, cheating each other since he was also determined to extract more work from her than that for which he paid. In those days he simply ignored the unkempt state of his home, and she ignored his meanness. Now, however, she toiled eagerly and efficiently, and he paid her generously. It made for a very satisfactory and cordial partnership, as well as a clean and well-run residence.

This evening Mrs. "D," as Scrooge fondly addressed her, delivered a message to Scrooge. Both she and he assumed it to be an invitation to dinner, or a fete of some sort, since he was included in many gatherings now, but it was nothing of the kind. Scrooge read the hand-written missive and was surprised at its contents.

> *My Dear Mr. Scrooge,*
>
> *Will you please do me and my daughter the honor of escorting us to the current performance of "The Untoward Suitor" at the Adelphi Theatre on Friday evening next. We will call for you in my carriage at 6:45 o'clock and will share supper, following.*
>
> *Your prompt reply will be appreciated, and I will accept no denial.*
>
> *Yours sincerely,*
> *Mrs. A. Sotherton.*

Scrooge was surprised and relieved that he had not offended Rebecca's mother to the extent that she wanted no more to do with him. Perhaps his note of apology had helped, or perhaps she was attempting to please her daughter by inviting him and was doing so with little enthusiasm of her own. Either way, Scrooge welcomed the invitation. He did not doubt that the evening would be pleasant since he enjoyed the company of both ladies very much. He would reply in the affirmative at once!

On the appointed date and time Scrooge was ready with his coat, hat, and gloves when Mrs. Sotherton's coachman approached his front entry door. Scrooge quickly climbed into the carriage and sat opposite the women as they exchanged happy greetings. Both admired him — one as his peer, and the other from a motherly perspective. He was an imposing figure and considered quite handsome for a person in his fifties, but it was his sincerity and sense of humor that generally won over his acquaintances, particularly those of the opposite gender. Men tended to be impressed, firstly, with his business acumen, and only later came to notice his other strengths of character.

Scrooge did not mention his clandestine departure from Mrs. Sotherton's afternoon soirée, since he had sent an apologetic note. Instead, they discussed various forms of music, Sir John Franklin's plan to navigate the Northwest Passage, and their young Queen. Scrooge was always amazed that these two ladies were willing to broach so many topics and were well-informed enough to make surprisingly compelling and sensible arguments. Unlike many women of their acquaintance, they actually read newspapers and discussed issues with several men in high places. Gossip over tea was not their sole means of forming opinions.

Upon their arrival at the Adelphi, Scrooge politely acted the role of escort and guided the women to their seats, knowing they did not actually require such assistance. Still, acting as chaperone to these particular women was a true pleasure, as well as an honor. After they were seated Scrooge scanned the audience and spotted several of his acquaintances, nodding to those who noticed him. One or two of them raised an eyebrow in recognition of Scrooge's companions, curious as to how he managed to be in such excellent company – and sitting in preferred seats, at that. He would no doubt be questioned by several people during the upcoming days.

The gas lights had been lit and turned up to a degree that best illuminated the actors, and soon the play began. Scrooge was enjoying the first several moments when, of a sudden, a woman glided gracefully onto center stage. As a magnet, her first few lines pulled the entire audience's attention to herself. She looked familiar, and he gasped when he realized who she was.

Why, of course! It's that impertinent Emma Aldrich, who cornered me at Mrs. Sotherton's! He admitted to himself that she was an excellent actress, but that was no surprise, considering what he had observed at the salon. He made a quick side glance at Mrs. Sotherton, to see if she had sensed his reaction, but could discern no change in her expression. She seemed to be merely enjoying the performance. Hopefully she was not aware that Scrooge held little esteem for this actress and that her outlandish behavior had been the final absurdity that sent him flying out Mrs. Sotherton's door and into the street!

Since he had not attended the theatre until eighteen months ago, and not often since then, Scrooge did not want to forego any pleasure of the evening, so he managed to set aside his opinion of Miss Aldrich and simply enjoy the play. He and his two companions laughed and sighed in unison, which must confirm that they were a good set. That evening each one became even more convinced that they could easily spend time together and that it would be time well employed.

After what seemed only a few moments, the curtain came down for the interlude. Per common etiquette, Scrooge made himself available to accompany the women wherever they wished to go, whether it be to remain in their seats or retire to the dress circle foyer. Both had stood and indicated a desire to move about a bit, which was what he had hoped.

The foyer was awash with similar theatre-goers who were seeking to stretch their legs or find some refreshment. While Scrooge secured something from the saloon, Mrs. Sotherton and Mrs. Langstone were surrounded by admiring men and women who either simply said hello or stood with them long enough to trade a few pleasantries. Scrooge and several of his acquaintances exchanged greetings before he was accosted by Mrs. Honora Purdy, who did not mind a bit that it was known to the Town's entire population that she was completely besotted with Ebenezer Scrooge. Mrs. Purdy was a widow whose husband's wealth and social standing had ensured the same status for her following his death, but her behavior could be somewhat odd. Upon espying Scrooge, she made for him at a lope, emitting her usual "hee-haw" that, in her case, stood for a laugh. She couldn't help it. Where others would snigger or titter, she would bray.

"Ah-heh, Mr. Scrooge," she snorted. "I haven't seen you in donkey's years, and I am that pleased to find you here, tonight. Are you alone?" He was relieved to be able to say he was not, and that, in fact, he needed to quickly return to his companions. She was disappointed and made no attempt to disguise it, leaving him with the promise that they would see each other again, and he would yet partner her in a dance! Scrooge smiled politely and made his way back to the easier pleasantries of Mrs. Sotherton and Mrs. Langstone.

Several people were still surrounding his two companions and Scrooge suspected that two or three of the men near Mrs. Langstone might be potential suitors. Both women were "holding court" quite well, which created an uneasiness in Scrooge. He had not seriously considered the fact that he might have competition for Mrs. Langstone's attention, much less her affection, and he found he was troubled by the thought. No, not merely troubled – he was jealous. Could he ask her if she was being pursued by anyone? Not under any circumstances, since the two of them had no understanding.

The performance was beyond Scrooge's expectations and it ended on a marvelously satirical note, which pleased the entire audience. Miss Aldrich's acting ability had put it over and she was required to bow several times before being allowed to quit the stage. As they all stood for their departure, Mrs. Sotherton announced, "Since she is an acquaintance, I am of a mind to visit Miss Aldrich backstage." Scrooge recoiled at the thought of facing the actress again, but there was nothing for it but to follow along since he was their escort. As they made their way to the dressing room he prayed that Miss Aldrich would not recall their earlier introduction and would not approach him with the boldness he had witnessed at the home of Mrs. Sotherton.

The door to Miss Aldrich's dressing room was wide open due to the number of admirers who wished to congratulate her. Scrooge was overjoyed by the size of the crowd, hoping it meant they would be forced to leave without making contact with the audacious actress, but it was not to be. Even though they were standing well to the rear of the hoard, she somehow spotted Scrooge and immediately "parted the waters" of her devotees, to make a way for them to enter. Within half a minute they found themselves not three feet from the dratted woman, who had focused her total attention on only one person in the room, heedless of the fact that she might be treating others with rudeness.

"Mr. Scrooge! How delighted I am to see you!" She placed both hands on her hips and announced, "You see, we have found each other again. It is often that way when two people are destined to be in each other's company." Pulling him aside, she lowered her voice only slightly and said, "You are a difficult man to forget, though I admit I made absolutely no attempt to do so." Her smile was ominous, as was Mrs. Langstone's countenance as she observed them.

Sensing danger, Mrs. Sotherton intervened by saying they were on their way to supper and must leave without lingering, but it did no good. In fact, it made matters worse.

"Supper, you say? What a delightful idea! I will cancel my earlier plans and join you. Just give me a few moments to change, and we shall be off. Where are we to dine? Never mind. It matters not to me, as long as I can enjoy this delightful man's company the entire time." Placing her hand on Scrooge's arm, she murmured loud enough that the others could hear, "I have missed you."

Supper was a disaster. The food was delectable, but the group was at sixes and sevens. Miss Aldrich was unbothered by anyone else's discomfort and attended solely to seeking the pleasure she found in the company of Ebenezer Scrooge. Her intentions were blatant, and she would not be put off, regardless of interruptions. More than once Mrs. Sotherton tried to introduce a topic of conversation in order to divert Miss Aldrich, but the actress would brook no subject other than her precious Mr. Scrooge and their "amore."

As Scrooge attempted to take a bite of food, she leaned in. "Now, my dear, how do you find the duck? Is it not absolutely decadent?" He was beginning to perspire and needed to breathe more easily, so he put down his fork and hooked his index finger between his neck and his collar. As he did so, she laid her hand on his knee and the unexpected intimacy sent him flying as if he had been stung by a wasp! He sprang from his chair, upsetting two glasses, and immediately found himself standing alone, with absolutely no explanation for it.

Two waiters rushed to the table to mop up the spill. "I do beg your pardon," Scrooge cried, "but every so often the muscle in my calf decides to cramp and I find I must stand and walk a bit, until the spasm eases. Please excuse me while I do so. I shall return anon." He was not a liar and hated the fact that he had just told an untruth, but in his alarm, it had just popped out!

Naturally, Miss Aldrich relished having the power to make Scrooge jump like a jack in the box, and she would never be deterred by such a silly antic. It only made him more of a challenge. Mrs. Langstone found his behavior, and his explanation for it, somewhat peculiar since his leg had never cramped during the times they had spent in each other's company.

While Scrooge wandered the nether regions of the restaurant, Miss Aldrich began a soliloquy, delivering her lines to perfection. "I find it so refreshing when a man plays diffident and pretends there is no attachment, simply to protect a woman's reputation." Ignoring the horrified glance that passed between Mrs. Sotherton and her daughter, she continued. "Mr. Scrooge is definitely a gentleman in that regard, and it only endears him to me all the more!" With that, she took a dainty bite of her confit, smiling sweetly as she chewed.

Both Mrs. Sotherton and Mrs. Langstone were visibly upset by the time Scrooge returned to the table, and the supper was rushed to its end, which disappointed Miss Aldrich. What was meant to have been the pleasure of sharing an excellent entrée, followed by a superb blancmange, had become a meal of discomfort and suspicion, and the party did not linger at the table once the supper was completed. Instead, Mrs. Sotherton ordered her carriage to be brought around as quickly as possible.

Miss Aldrich was the first to be delivered to her residence, and Scrooge, as dictated by polite society, escorted her to the door. The other women watched in cold silence as Miss Aldrich leaned her head on his shoulder and clung to him at the entrance, not wanting to part with him.

Scrooge managed to pry her fingers from his arm as he remarked, "I thank you for a very enjoyable performance this evening, and for a most interesting supper." *If I see you in future I shall dash to the other side of the street. I would prefer to chance being squashed flat by a runaway cab than subject myself to such wiles!* With that thought churning in his brain, he bowed slightly before turning her to face the entryway and propelling her very gently, but firmly, through the door.

Once back in the carriage, Scrooge and his companions rode on in exceedingly uncomfortable silence. Miss Aldrich was correct in saying that Scrooge was a gentleman because he was too much of one to say what was on his mind. His companions were too upset to say anything at all, lest they say too much, or worse, discover more than they wanted to know. Each was consumed by his or her particular sentiments, and it wouldn't do to discuss any of them.

Scrooge was thoroughly disgusted with himself for not having been better able to counter the behavior of Miss Aldrich, and he was outraged at her intrusiveness and impertinence. If the actress were a man, he would have called him out for such impolite behavior!

Mrs. Sotherton, on the other hand, was quite overcome with guilt. She was, after all, responsible for the entire debacle, and none of this would have occurred had she not introduced Miss Aldrich into the mix. She did not for a moment believe that the actress and Scrooge were in any way connected, which only increased her guilt over what he had endured this evening. She was also responsible for subjecting Rebecca to a show of coarse advances toward a man she truly admired. It was all too, too bad. Mrs. Sotherton sincerely wished she could give herself a very painful swift kick!

Mrs. Langstone was hurt, and somewhat doubtful. She did not want to believe that Scrooge could ever have ties with such a woman, but the actions of this evening suggested otherwise. It would be a simple matter to address him as he sat across from her in the carriage, and ask, "Mr. Scrooge, are you in any way connected with Miss Aldrich?", but that would be ill-mannered and similar to something Miss Aldrich would ask. In addition, he would, of course, make a denial, and she would be no better off because her fears would now include the possibility that he might also be a liar. Oh, if only she were alone in her bedchamber and could allow the tears to flow.

CHAPTER FOUR

Mrs. Adelaide Sotherton

On the Monday morning following the play, Scrooge received a message from Mrs. Sotherton.

Dear Mr. Scrooge,

I must apologise for the outcome of Friday night's event and beg your pardon for placing you and my daughter in a very uncomfortable situation. I do assure you it was not done purposefully. I have also apologised to Rebecca, but I fear I may have caused a breach between the two of you that only you can mend, even though the fault was not yours.

As you know, I entertain unconventional characters as a diversion for myself, but this time I have harmed others in my enjoyment of them. I suppose we are never too old to learn, and I have learnt a lesson in this. I pray you will forgive my thoughtlessness and continue to be my valued friend.

To that end, may I request that you visit me on Tuesday, at 4:00 o'clock. I will serve you tea without all

29

of the hubbub, and we two may have a pleasant conversation.

Most Sincerely,
A. Sotherton

Scrooge was very appreciative of Mrs. Sotherton's sentiments and knew them to be sincere, but he was concerned about his relationship with Mrs. Langstone. What should he do? He would hopefully come up with a way to broach the subject, but meanwhile he must reply to Mrs. Sotherton, which he did immediately.

Dear Mrs. Sotherton,

I am in receipt of your letter and very much appreciate it. However, you do not owe me an apology since you did nothing blameworthy. If there has been a breach created between your daughter and me I am certain it can be mended, and I will proceed in that direction. Meanwhile, esteemed lady, please be assured of our friendship and what I pray will be continued good times in future.

I gratefully accept your invitation to tea, and I look forward to an enjoyable interview.

Yours, in Sincerity,
E. Scrooge

Although she had not said as much, it seemed to Scrooge that Mrs. Sotherton was not taken in by the antics of Miss Aldrich, and for that he was very grateful. He only hoped he could somehow convince Rebecca that there was no connection between him and the actress!

CR80

Scrooge appeared at Mrs. Sotherton's home as summoned, and noted how soothing the rooms were without all the commotion. He suspected that his hostess would invite fewer outlandish personages to her home in future, if for no other reason than that she had come to view the behaviors of some of them as a liability. It had been proven so at supper, not four days earlier.

"Mr. Scrooge, my friend," said Mrs. Sotherton, greeting him warmly. "Thank you for accepting my invitation. Please sit there so that we can face each other and not only share tea, but also converse more easily."

Seating himself, Scrooge said, "I was very pleased to hear from you, and I apologize for anything I may have done to bring about such an unhappy end to what began as quite the merry outing." He regretted his words the moment he said them because she was convinced that it had all been her doing, and he did not wish to add to her guilt. So, he added, "You had no way of knowing the tricks and subterfuge Miss Aldrich would employ, and I believe we were all her victims." He frowned, and said, "I fail to see, however, what she expected to gain by such behavior."

"I believe I know," said Mrs. Sotherton. "I have observed that most unhappy people try to make others unhappy too, and she not only attempted to create a breach between you and Rebecca, she hoped you might even find her advances irresistible. Some men would, you know."

It was difficult to comprehend, yet he knew it to be so. He had even found her attractive, and admitted to himself that, had she been more ladylike, he would have found her more appealing. Not in preference to Rebecca, however. Never! The two did not compare.

A maid brought the tea tray, sat it on a table and departed when Mrs. Sotherton said she would pour.

"And now, Mr. Scrooge, rather than use our time to slowly arrive at what is on both our minds, I will begin by saying I know you are curious as to why I pursue the company of persons who often flaunt the rules of society. In answering, I must first admit that I find them somewhat entertaining, but I now believe there is also a danger with some, as we have seen."

Scrooge nodded slightly as she continued. "You would have a right to ask why I find such persons to be of interest, considering the trials you recently experienced at the hands of one of them, but to fully answer the question, I need to go back in time. I hope you won't mind the reminiscences of an older woman, but it may prove informative." She poured him a cup of tea, offered him a bun, and they both settled back.

"I was nineteen when my father decided I should marry, and he had already chosen the fellow. He did not mind whether I would be satisfied with the man, or not, but had decided on him as a matter of wealth and breeding. Ha! As if that were the measure of a man! It was how he measured men, however, and I was forced to marry someone I did not love, whose company did not appeal in any aspect, and whom I found to be wholly lacking in good character. He ignored me much of the time (for which I was usually grateful); drank and gambled away a good portion of his fortune; and was eventually thrown from a horse that neither he, nor anyone else, could control. His neck was broken, and he died immediately. I was not yet twenty-five years old, with a very young child — Rebecca — who was the sun and the moon to me." She paused, as if deciding whether or not to share all, and proceeded.

"I cannot tell you how relieved I was when the local vicar came to tell me that my husband was dead. I wanted to shout for joy, and should be ashamed to admit it, but I do not mind saying so to you at this time of my life. It was as if I had been gloriously released from a dungeon where I was held in heavy chains, with absolutely no hope of ever making an escape.

"Rather than bore you with too many details, I will simply say that I eventually met Mr. Sotherton, who possessed all of the wealth, breeding and power my father had sought, but he was also a fine man. His were true virtues, and we had a wonderful life together." She smiled and said, "I realize this has not addressed the original question, but here is the answer you seek.

"After the death of my first husband, while I was yet a young widow, I experienced an independence I had never known, and I sought persons of less restrictive behavior. I enjoyed their lack of caution and their brazen refusal to be ordered about by others, but lest you think I became like them, let me assure you that my enjoyment was always that of an excellent observer. Still, it became a habit, and at various times I wanted to be in the company of such characters to prove, I suppose, that I was, at last, a free woman!"

Scrooge must ask, "And how did Mr. Sotherton take to that, after you married?"

"He was not as entertained as I, but he did not altogether disapprove. I believe he saw the dangers and he preferred that I keep such gatherings to a minimum, which I did." Pursing her lips, she added, "I have decided, following our debacle with Miss Aldrich, that observing persons who have little or no self-control at a salon is one thing, but inviting them to attend more intimate gatherings can be abject recklessness." Neither of them said as much, but the fact was that Mrs. Sotherton had not invited Miss Aldrich to accompany them even so far as the stage door. Miss Aldrich had invited herself.

Scrooge knew, from her reputation, that during her second marriage Mrs. Sotherton had become powerful in her own right, and she continued to exert a great deal of influence in the social and political spheres of London. It was ironic that she should have such power when she was one to disregard any stringent rule she considered absurd. No one would question her, however, because she was so well established, and also because she was of an age that her viewpoint was based on a good many years of experience. Her well-stated arguments contained a surfeit of history, as well as logic, against which many younger adversaries could not effectively argue.

There was one other issue Mrs. Sotherton wished to address. "Mr. Scrooge, I am aware that my daughter thinks highly of you, and I believe it is mutual. I have apologized to her for allowing the actions of Miss Aldrich to plant seeds of doubt in her mind where you are concerned, and I have reassured her that you met the actress only once, right here at my salon, shame on me! She knows I always speak the truth, and I pray that has helped her to sort things in her mind, but the next step will, unfortunately, be yours. I deeply regret placing the two of you in this position, but I am confident it can be rectified."

Scrooge hoped so. Once again, he reassured her that she had done nothing for which to chastise herself and that he believed all would be well. That having been said, they spoke of other things, finished their tea, and Scrooge rose to leave. She offered her hand and he bowed as he took it, just before she surprised him by patting him lightly, and very fondly, on the cheek.

"Good luck to you, my friend," said she as he stepped from the room. They had each been encouraged by the conversation and both had hopes regarding Scrooge and Rebecca Langstone.

CHAPTER FIVE

Rebecca Langstone

J
ulian and Marian Thorne had chosen a fine evening for a musicale. Scrooge was looking forward to it very much, not only for the enjoyment of the performances, but the company in which he was bound to find himself. For decades, because of the scope of his business, Scrooge had known, and been known by, most of the businessmen and gentlemen in London, so it was likely he would find himself among friends and acquaintances. At one time they would have shied away from the very sight of him, not wishing to be brought down by his meanness, but that was no longer the case. At gatherings these days he was sought out for conversation and lively bantering. Two years ago, Scrooge would not have been invited to the event and, had he been, he would most certainly have refused. In those days he would have considered such frivolity a waste of his time since it would garner him no monetary profit.

Scrooge was easily meandering through the crowd, greeting and speaking with various acquaintances, when he spotted Ira Thorne across the room. Ira was Julian's father and Scrooge's avowed adversary. Scrooge had dealt with Thorne on a legal matter not eighteen months earlier and had bested him, yet had treated Thorne fairly, and with respect. Still, even with the clemency Scrooge had shown, they had not parted well, and Scrooge suspected that Thorne continued to harbor ill feeling. So, he was surprised when their eyes met, and Thorne raised his glass, then nodded. Scrooge knew that was as much as he would get from the fellow, but it was enough, and it spoke volumes from such a proud man as Ira Thorne. Scrooge's nephew, Fred, was particular friends with Julian Thorne, and surely that had played a part in softening the senior Thorne's heart.

The music was about to begin, which meant Scrooge should find a seat. He preferred the back of the room, but was forced to sit closer to the front. In the distance he heard a quick "hee-haw" from Honora Purdy, and immediately sought seating in the opposite direction. He spotted three open chairs and was deciding whether to take one or stand in the back, when he felt a light touch on his arm. "Shall we sit together?" Fearing it was Mrs. Purdy, he steeled himself to turn and reply. It was Mrs. Langstone, however, and he had never been more delighted to see her. They had not spoken since the debacle following the play some days ago, and he was anxious to set things to rights, if possible. Her invitation suggested to him that it may be. Or was she simply being polite, since he was blocking the way?

"If you don't mind," she said, "I apologize, but I should sit on the outside chair since I am to play the pianoforte and it would make it less disruptive when I approach the piano." So, they claimed two seats closer to the instrument, with Mrs. Langstone on the aisle. Neither was concerned with seating protocol and preferred, instead, to operate according to utility – within limits, of course.

Scrooge was impressed with the news that Mrs. Langstone would perform. "I was unaware that you played", said he, but quickly followed that statement with, "Well, I presumed you had learnt to play early on, as most young girls do, but I did not realize you were a performer. I beg your pardon for not asking before now. Had I known, I would have insisted you honor me with some Bach, or perhaps Schuman. What do you play for us, this evening?"

"Marian has asked me to play a Chopin Valse." Smiling, Mrs. Langstone admitted, "I have spent the past two weeks preparing and could not seem to commit to perfect memory two of the more difficult passages, so I am forced to read from the musical score. Marian has assured me I will not be chastised for doing so, since this is a private recital." He was certain she would make a grand impression, sheet music or no, and was looking forward to hearing her play. More than that, he was anxious to speak to her concerning the dreadful Miss Emma Aldrich, but that could wait.

The performances were a success, as might have easily been predicted. Marian Thorne preferred an eclectic evening of music and chose her players accordingly. A very accomplished young artist performed her own composition on the violin, and then Mrs.

Langstone played the Chopin piece without flaw. As she bowed to the applause, Scrooge wished he could stand and announce to the assembly, "Mrs. Langstone is my particular friend. Is she not the epitome of loveliness and perfection?" Then a well-known mezzo-soprano sang a popular old English folk song a cappella, and a popular tenor graced the room with a Verdi aria, accompanied by his own pianist.

As the accolades died down, Marian Thorne approached the front of the room to announce that the entertainment had been concluded. Before the guests could stir, however, a male voice boomed from the back, "And now, please, may we hear a four-handed piece from Mrs. Langstone and Mrs. Thorne? Mightn't we?" The women were surprised at the request, but the cries of agreement encouraged them, and they settled on an exuberant tune they both knew – one they had performed together a time before. Their performance roused the guests to a level of gaiety that left the house in very high spirits.

When the applause had died down an excited gentleman rushed to Mrs. Langstone's side to offer his congratulations, and to stand a bit too close, as far as Scrooge was concerned. Scrooge was already a bit off balance where his relationship with Rebecca Langstone was concerned, and a stab of envy, as well as fear, forced him to approach them and offer her his arm. She took it as she politely excused herself to the man, who bowed slightly as he allowed them to pass. Scrooge hoped the fellow could see that he was imposing himself on another man's patch, even though that was not quite the case, since Scrooge and Mrs. Langstone had not come to any sort of understanding.

A large buffet was laid out in the spacious dining room and guests began to drift that way. Scrooge and Mrs. Langstone remained together, even though each was aware of a vague breach that threatened their future. Together they partook of bits of food and merely picked at them, since neither had any particular appetite.

Both were recalling their evening with Miss Aldrich and they were still amazed at the ability of one person to threaten the well-being of others with merely a few well-chosen statements and actions. Whereas Scrooge and Mrs. Sotherton knew full well what the actress was about, Mrs. Langstone was in the opposing position. She had been the intended object to be "got rid of" after all, and Scrooge was uncertain of the success of Miss Aldrich's plan. He needed to know, but was unsure of how to ask.

Finally, Scrooge requested that Mrs. Langstone take a turn with him, and as they walked he guided her to an outside terrace. Others had made the same discovery on such a fine evening, but they eventually located a corner where they could speak privately. As is often the case when there is a topic that must be raised following an uneasy silence, both began to speak at the same time. It did ease their apprehensions somewhat, because it made them laugh. Mrs. Langstone finally convinced him to begin first, and so he did, after swallowing hard and praying that he would find the right words. He looked about, to ensure that no one was within hearing distance before using her given name.

"Rebecca, please allow me to beg your pardon for ruining our evening at the theatre. I am shamefaced by what appeared to be an intimate connection between Miss Aldrich and myself. It was a dreadful situation and I regret that you and your mother were placed in such an awkward position." He shifted on his feet before saying, "But I must add something else. Lest you believe her insinuations, I am not even acquainted with the woman, other than meeting her once at your mother's salon, a week earlier." Mrs. Langstone did not move and simply watched him intently, which caused him to begin to over-explain and run his statements together.

"What I am trying to tell you, Rebecca, is that there is no connection between me and that woman. I realize it may not make a difference to you one way or another, and I cannot assume that it would, but I am determined to save our friendship if it is at all possible because it is very important to me, and if that evening suggested to you that I was lacking in the sort of character you require in a friend . . ." Here she interrupted him in an effort to rescue him from himself.

"It's alright, Ebenezer. I have spoken with my mother and everything has been explained. In addition, I have eyes, and I could see which one of you was misbehaving. Your statements tonight have only further confirmed to me that you are the same man I believed you to be. I will admit that it was an embarrassing situation, but I also admit that I admire the gentlemanly way you responded to such an onslaught of inappropriate attention. Even now, you assume responsibility rather than attempt to blacken Miss Aldrich's name. So, you see, my belief in your good character is intact, and we remain friends."

Mrs. Langstone did not admit how hurt she had been and that she had, for a short time, questioned his veracity. She had even asked herself whether it might be best if she entertained the attentions of other men who were desirous of her company. In the end, she wisely applied what she knew of Ebenezer Scrooge, thought things through and discussed the incident with her mother. Tonight, after speaking with him face-to-face, she was finally able to put her unpleasant imaginations to rest.

Scrooge's relief was almost palpable. He took a deep breath that puffed his chest somewhat, held it a moment and said, "Well then, I thank you for your generosity of mind, and will say no more about it."

"Nor will I," said she, and each of them sincerely hoped they would never again come face to face with the very talented and extremely devious Miss Emma Aldrich.

Scrooge had come to the musicale in a cab, so he was appreciative and delighted when Mrs. Langstone offered to transport him home in her carriage. The evening had been a stunning success, as was generally the case when the younger Thornes entertained, and everyone was in good humor as they departed. Scrooge and Mrs. Langstone were pleased to have time alone in her carriage, and quickly fell into relaxed conversation.

"Rebecca, I hope you understand that I am very sincere when I say how impressed I am with your ability at the pianoforte. Your solo was glorious, and your duet with Marian Thorne near raised the roof! It was delightful, and I thank you for your willingness to entertain others with your talent."

Mrs. Langstone was grateful for his praise, but her natural humility would not allow her to preen. "I admit I was quite serious about my music as a young girl, and even as I grew older, but I cannot take credit and claim any proficiency is solely my own doing. All of the practice in the world would not make a whit of difference had I not been graced with a certain amount of God-given aptitude. For that reason, I will give praise where it is due." He knew she meant what she said, and that it was not a pretense of humility designed to draw more adulation.

"Even so," she continued, almost as if she were talking to herself, "performing is not always an easy thing for me. I have been approached, even this evening, to play in larger venues, but I do not wish to spend my time in practicing to the extent that it becomes a chore rather than a joy. Nor do I believe I could continually perform on stage before large audiences of critical strangers. I have not the heart for it. I am comfortable in smaller settings and more intimate environs."

Mrs. Langstone's willingness to expose her innermost thoughts endeared her to Scrooge all the more, yet he was unable to admit that he might be absolutely in love. The very notion and the practice of romance had eluded him for so long that it was an inclination quite foreign to his thinking. His heart had only recently been unlocked, much less flung wide open.

But, wait! What was that she said? He must ask.

"Rebecca, please forgive me if I am prying, but who was the gentleman who approached you tonight after you and Marian played your duet? Was he offering you the opportunity to play professionally?" Hopefully she did not detect the actual motive and the fear behind his question.

"Why, yes, he was. That was Mr. Harris, and he has made the offer more than once, but I have said no each time. I assume he believes I am simply being coy, even though I have attempted to convince him that I am genuinely not at all interested."

Ah! Then, he was not a suitor, after all! Scrooge was vastly relieved, for a man who could not admit that he might be in love.

Mrs. Langstone continued. "You know, Ebenezer, all of this talk of spending so many hours at the piano brings to mind a time when I quit the instrument altogether and did not expect ever to return to anything that might bring joy. I will say that I am grateful to have been brought through that period in my life and been able to return to the things that bring happiness, not only to me, but hopefully also to others, even if it is on a small scale." He believed he knew of the time to which she referred, but asked, "Do you allude to the abduction of your son?"

"Yes," she replied, wistfully. "I do not often speak of it, and then only with very few of my associates, but you are different in that you have a good heart and you truly care about the troubles of others. Yet, you somehow manage to remain practical in the face of sorrow, and often that is exactly what is needed, is it not?" He appreciated her remarks and nodded his understanding.

In 1829 Mrs. Langstone's six-year-old son, Peter, had been abducted while in his nanny's care on an outing to the park, and his body was recovered from the Thames two weeks later. It was the most heartbreaking time for Mrs. Langstone and her husband who, four years later, succumbed to basically what she and most everyone else, including his physician, considered a broken heart. She had eventually recovered enough to get on with life, and even to enjoy it, but the loss was something she would never "get over," as some people at the time had politely hinted she should do. Scrooge would never admonish her with such statements, which she greatly appreciated. She did not know that for some time it had been his earnest desire to somehow assist in solving the mystery of her son's abduction and death, even though he knew that would be a near impossible undertaking.

Without thinking, Scrooge took her hand and held it. It was a gesture they both needed, and they maintained the contact until he saw her to her door before returning to the carriage, to be driven to his own door by her coachman.

CHAPTER SIX

Priscilla Wilkins

Scrooge was extremely happy with his life, yet something was still amiss. The only sort of love he was not practicing these days was romantic love, but in all other forms of caring he was definitely a reformed man. No one was more charitable than he, and his family and employees were always well looked after, even to the extreme. He was unaware of it, but his employees had occasionally faced insults from envious acquaintances whose employers were not so concerned with their well-being. So, love, itself, wasn't the problem. These days he was a lover in every way, save one, but it wasn't as if he had never known romance, for he had. Once. There had been Belle. Young, beautiful Belle.

Scrooge's courtship of Belle had ended so long ago that he had no idea about such attachments later in life, particularly those of long standing, as in marriage. He was such a young pup when he loved Belle

— full of the exuberance and ignorance that can make those years so wonderful. At that age there was very little that was tried and true, since one had not lived long enough to "try" anything for very long, much less test its truth.

During Scrooge's courtship of Belle, he discovered that he had the talent to be a successful businessman. He could make money faster and more easily than most, and it gradually took control of his thinking, eventually becoming his life's force. Nothing and no one else mattered − not his sister, not the victims of his greed (since he did not mind injuring others for a few pounds silver), and not even Belle. He had fallen in love, instead, with wealth and the power it bought.

Belle saw it first, and she confronted him with the fact that another idol — his love of money — had replaced her. Her words, "I release you, with a full heart, for the love of him you once were," were painful to hear, but by then he was so committed to his quest for worldly success that he foolishly let her go. At the time he reckoned she was too short-sighted to share his vision and that she did not understand the importance of his plans, or his success. That, alone, would make her an inappropriate partner, or so he convinced himself before forgetting her altogether as the gleam from another coin caught his eye, instead.

In the ensuing years Scrooge amassed more wealth and power, using none of it to help anyone, even himself. In fact, his love of mankind diminished steadily in direct proportion to the wealth he accumulated. His downward spiral of greed and meanness eventually spun out of control, earning him the moniker Ira Thorne once gave him — "Mr. Scourge." The worst thing about him in those years was his unawareness of how wicked he had become. As with many corrupt persons, he assumed the rest of mankind was made up of fools, which meant they were worthless, and his actions were therefore moved by that opinion. They were insects, meant to be stepped on.

Things were completely different now. Scrooge's life was in such good order and so rewarding to himself and others that he could simply enjoy his family and acquaintances for the rest of his life. So why did he feel something was yet missing? An intelligent being, he knew what it was, but he did not want to admit it to himself because that would mean he must make up his mind sooner, rather than later. He told himself he was too old. He was too set in his ways. He was too busy. He was too . . . afraid.

Following one of Scrooge's evenings of reflections on several subjects, including his relationship with Mrs. Langstone, Marley materialized. He remained only long enough to say, "Do not be guided by fear, Ebenezer. Be guided by faith.", and he quickly departed. Rather, he dissolved into thin air, since Marley never came and went as a normal person would do. He had not given Scrooge the opportunity to discuss anything. Perhaps he would brook no argument. It was a simple truth, and there could be no "on the other hand."

For several days Scrooge recalled Marley's visit and was struck by the fact that it had come on the heels of Scrooge's ruminations on the subject of romance, among other things. Now, what to do? Marley was nowhere in sight and Scrooge would rather not discuss it with his family, nor could he consult the men in the counting-house. There was always the Rector, but he suspected he needed the assistance of a woman.

Certainly not Rebecca Langstone, nor her mother, Mrs. Sotherton. Who, then? He thought through the list of his female acquaintances. Marian Thorne? No. She was too young, and Scrooge was not well enough acquainted with her. Definitely not Honora Purdy, who was, herself, taken with Scrooge!

Priscilla Wilkins? Yes! Priscilla was the wife of his good friend Dick Wilkins, with whom Scrooge had been a young apprentice at Old Fezziwig's. These days both Dick and Priscilla were his close friends, and Scrooge knew her to be direct, trustworthy and wise. He would see her this week, no matter how much he felt a fool. She would not belittle him for his inexperience at such an awkward age! Scrooge sat down and quickly dispatched a note.

> *My Dear Priscilla,*
>
> *I pray you will grant me permission to impose upon your good nature. I find I am in need of your advice on a topic that I cannot — will not — discuss with anyone else. Naturally, I would not insist that Dick absent himself from the conversation, but I am seeking your company in particular because you are a wise woman, a good friend, and you do not gossip. I await your reply concerning a convenient date and time, and I thank you in advance.*
>
> *Yours Sincerely,*
> *Ebenezer S.*

The following day Scrooge received a response from Priscilla:

> *My Dear Ebenezer,*
>
> *I am gratified to be chosen as your confidante and will happily receive you on Tuesday at 3:30 o'clock. I must confess I am anxious to know what we are to*

discuss. Meanwhile, I will prepare a very nice tea for you. Dick is not invited.

Yours Sincerely,
Priscilla

Priscilla always served one of the best teas in London, and Scrooge had been looking forward to her cook's delicacies for three days. Sharing such comforts would perhaps ease them into what he feared may prove to be a rather difficult conversation, for him.

CஐஇD

"Now, Ebenezer," prodded Priscilla as she poured his second cup of a lovely brew and offered him another pastry, "we have spoken of your business and Fred and Catherine, but I suspect we have not come close to the topic you hoped to broach. Are you now able, with a full stomach, to tell it to me?"

To brace himself, Scrooge took a large swallow of tea but, in his agitation, he took a breath at the same time and began to cough uncontrollably. He stood up, covered his mouth and nose with his napkin, and marched around the room. He barked and wheezed, put his head down, then up and down again until he was able to breathe, but he could barely speak. Through gasps he managed to croak, "You . . . must . . . believe me, Priscilla . . . this was not . . . a planned . . . tactic designed . . . to . . . put you off," and they both laughed, although Scrooge's laughter sounded more like the honk of a wild goose.

Within several moments Scrooge had collected himself enough to sit and converse, and so he began.

"Priscilla, I am, for all intents and purposes, an old man. I'm far too old to be having this conversation, but my youth and adulthood were wasted largely in the pursuit of tangible profit rather than the benefits that come from right relationships with others. Because of all that wasted time, I find I am a bit unprepared for what now faces me."

"And what would that be?", asked Priscilla. She was truly curious.

Oh, dear. Well, in for a penny, in for a pound. This is why you are here old boy, so forge ahead!

He didn't know how else to say it. "I need to know about love, my friend." Her raised eyebrows spurred him on. "I am not speaking of the sort of love we should all bestow on our fellow man. I speak of romance. I know little to nothing about it, you see. Due to my decades of thinking only of myself, I am totally unacquainted with Cupid and his impetuous firing of arrows."

Priscilla hadn't known what to expect from Scrooge when he suggested they meet, but it was not this. Although such an action would have been impolite in most company, she was relaxed enough with this man that she puffed out her cheeks, holding the air a moment before slowly letting it out. Several questions came to mind, but she settled on one, suspecting she already knew the answer.

"And do you have anyone in particular in mind, when you speak of romance?"

Scrooge leaned forward. "Priscilla, I am relying on your complete discretion regarding this conversation, but if I hadn't confidence in you, I would not be sitting here." He took a fortifying breath and said, "I am certain you are aware of my particular friendship with Mrs.

Langstone, and my regard for her." He saw her nod and continued. "The problem is that I have a tender attachment to her, but I am not certain about love. I do not know much about its properties, and I certainly could not say it exists between me and Mrs. Langstone. I should add that I am unpracticed in the art, would possibly not understand how it feels, and I do not know if I am capable of the depth and sort of love a woman requires. Nor am I convinced, at my age, that I should pursue it, even if it turns out to be the true proverbial passion." He closed his eyes and shook his head, "I am not making sense. Can you pull anything worthwhile from this muddle I have just handed you?"

"I certainly can," reassured Priscilla. She was very fond of this dear friend, and she knew he was sailing in what was, for him, an uncharted ocean. She surprised him by beginning with the very thing Marley had last said.

"Do not be overtaken by fear in this instance, Ebenezer, for the fear itself may prevent you from making any sort of decision, or it may take you in the wrong direction altogether. Let's be honest — it would be a very simple matter, were you one and twenty years old and knew nothing about the ups and downs of life. At that age you would simply follow your heart, but caution is one of the things we seem to grow into with the years, and an excess of caution can paralyze." She wanted to know something.

"Let me ask you, can you imagine a life without her in it?"

His answer was an immediate, "No, I cannot," and he followed it with another question. "But how on earth can one know, for certain, that the desire to be together will last?" The moment he voiced the trepidation he realized how boyish it sounded. It was the sort of thing he should have learnt ages ago.

Once again Priscilla surprised him by echoing Marley. "There are some things, my friend, that we have to take on faith. I had no idea what would face me, or us, when I married Dick, but I knew for certain that whatever it was, I wanted to face it with him." Scrooge looked somewhat doubtful and she addressed his facial expression by saying, "I know, I know. Those are brave words for facing the unknown when you are barely out of pinafores, but what is the alternative? What is life for you now? I know it is a very satisfying and happy life, but you want more, and it seems you want it with a certain person." His mien said that she had hit the mark, so, looking at him with fondness, she continued.

"I cannot tell you what to do Ebenezer, but if you decide not to pursue this matter to at least the next step, you will forfeit any hopes you now have of establishing something permanent and intimate. I like Mrs. Langstone very much, by the way, and have seen you together on several occasions. You seem to me to be very well suited. You do not have to marry tomorrow, or ever, but you are evidently at a crossroads in your mind and you must choose whether to end it now, or to test and prove — one way or the other — whether your attachment is real, and strong enough, to look to the future."

Now Scrooge must ask a particular question that his instincts said had no answer, as must be the case with many questions of love.

Nevertheless, he embarked by asking, "Priscilla, how does a woman's mind work? How does she see these things? What does she want?"

Priscilla couldn't resist, she had to laugh. "Oh, Ebenezer. If I knew how to answer all of that I could write it out and sell it to every man on earth at any price I wanted to name, and I would make my fortune!"

Scrooge knew she was not laughing at him and he realized the question was absurd, but it was the crux of the matter, was it not? Just as that thought occurred to him, Priscilla continued.

"My friend, I believe men and women want mostly the same things, it's just that we go about getting them in different ways. Women are constrained by social edicts that demand they be subtle, and their signals to men may be impossible for men to read. A man may do the opposite of what a woman desires simply because he is unable to recognize her intent, and she then interprets his actions as a rejection of her, rather than as a misunderstanding. I have seen more than one couple fall out over something trivial which, when acted on with high sensibilities, rather than good sense, took them to the breaking point."

"But how does that help me, Priscilla? How do I know how to read Mrs. Langstone?"

Without hesitation, Priscilla replied. "Mrs. Langstone is a very rational woman and I do not believe she would ever give mixed or confusing cues, but let's say she did, unintentionally. Once she realized you had got it wrong (and I believe she would realize it), I'm certain she would converse with you and make her intents understood." Here

Priscilla feared she was making things more confusing for her friend, so she decided on a different tact.

"Ebenezer, you cannot predict every nuance that will occur between two people, whether it be man-to-woman, woman-to-woman, or man-to-man, so do not attempt to formulate a schedule that you must follow when dealing with others, particularly in this situation with Mrs. Langstone. The proper approach will not always come from your head. At times it will come from your heart. I would advise you, however, not to let your heart always have the rule, either. Listen to it, but never forsake good sense."

There was one other thing Scrooge had said that Priscilla wanted to address. They were still nibbling on tarts and sipping tea, and the informality made certain aspects of the discussion easier.

"About your age . . . You are not, as you admit, growing any younger. None of us is. Therefore, you might also want to consider the fact that you do not have decades in which to be undecided. I cannot predict whether either of you would find someone else to love if you continued to hesitate, but that is a possibility." She smiled. "Do you see what I mean by faith? There is no way to answer every question that inserts itself into your mind, particularly if you are operating in fear, so you need to listen, at least in part, to your heart, and continue to believe. Perhaps a good place to start may be to test her feelings. Can you do that by declaring yourself, perhaps, at least to some extent?"

Scrooge was unable to pledge himself to such a course of action at the moment, but he did feel an inner push to do so. It was perhaps a matter of following both Priscilla's and Marley's advice to have more faith, but how could he have more faith without being certain of where his hopes lie?

Scrooge's conversation with Priscilla had helped him to see what he wanted a little more clearly, but things were still not entirely intelligible, and he did not yet have the courage to follow through. He told Priscilla as much before they moved on to a few other topics over another cup of tea and more of those heavenly pastries. Eventually he rose to leave, thanked her profusely, and bid her adieu. He had much to consider.

CHAPTER SEVEN

The Cargo in the Barge

Fred's trip to the Netherlands, and possibly Belgium or Denmark, would take a minimum of three weeks, perhaps longer. He made his apologies to Catherine, but he needn't have worried. Her response to his announcement that he was to be away had been simple. "Well, if you must go, I shall not attempt to prevent it. I will, however, request that upon your return you bless me with an evening at the opera, even though I know you will enjoy the performance to the same degree that I will enjoy keeping a half-empty house for several weeks! That, my good husband, will even the score!"

Catherine was not one to cling to her husband like some women she could name, but she was a bit ill-at-ease when he was away from home. On those rare occasions, every noise and draft increased at night, and the darkness was always a deeper black. She felt her solitary situation all the more since the servants slept in another part of the house and she was uncertain as to whether a scream would even reach their ears. Teague, her small Spaniel, stayed with her, of course, but he was no better than she at discerning sounds, and wherein she might quiver very quietly under her covers, Teague was apt to whimper pitifully from beneath the bed!

On a Friday near the end of May, Fred gave Catherine a loving kiss and a hug neither of them wanted to end. Finally, he bade her farewell and began his extended trip. He was extremely happy to be doing business and learning the intricacies of trade, but he truly loved and enjoyed being married to Catherine. He would sorely miss her.

CB80

It was a fine morning in the latter part of June that Scrooge entered the counting-house and greeted each worker before reaching his own office, to settle in. Before he could sit down, however, Cratchit approached and handed him a piece of paper.

"Mr. Scrooge, I do not wish to disturb you the moment you arrive, but we have received a message from a Mr. Goll at the Paddington Basin. It seemed somewhat urgent."

Scrooge quickly scanned the note and said, "They are holding one of our barge shipments from Aylesbury, but they do not state why. They request my presence at the Basin, to deal with the problem before they will unload. I must do it now, it seems. Cratchit, you remain here and tend to business. Homer, on with your hat. You may accompany me to see what sort of nonsense these people have with us." They easily found a cab that sped them to the Paddington Basin, where they were directed to Mr. Goll, the wharfinger.

"Ah, Mr. Scrooge, I have been looking for you, and when you see our problem you will understand why I have also asked a police constable to attend us." As Mr. Goll completed his sentence, a tall rugged constable strolled toward them, smiling in recognition as he greeted Scrooge. Scrooge and Constable Rollo Norris were well acquainted, having been involved in the case of a burglary and attempted arson at the counting-house several months earlier. Norris's greeting to Homer was much less enthusiastic, which was owing to the fact that both he and Homer were vying for the attentions of Bob Cratchit's eldest daughter, Martha.

Homer Probert had established a friendly attachment with Martha first, and had hopes of a permanent alliance until Norris was called in on the day of the burglary – a day when Martha was delivering a doctor's receipt to her father for Tiny Tim – and was, himself, instantly smitten. Giving no thought to Homer or the hopes he might have, Rollo was now pursuing her acquaintance. Homer was doing his best to thwart any progress Rollo might make with lovely Martha and was finding it extremely difficult to behave civilly toward the "Peeler," as Sir Robert Peel's police constables were often called.

Mr. Goll addressed Scrooge. "Now, Sir, this may be a bit upsetting, but I am bound to show you what we discovered amongst the shipment." As if to reassure Scrooge, he added, "Since you only hired the craft, it's nothing to do with you in terms of culpability. However, we do need to get to the truth of the matter and we'd best begin with you, since you arranged the shipment and its delivery." Scrooge wondered what could be occurring that would suggest anyone's culpability, but he knew from many years in business that it was rarely anything so serious that it could not be sorted with the application of some sensible thinking.

Within minutes they arrived at the barge, which was still laden with most of its shipment of leather and paper. Tucked in among the cargo was a bundle unlike the others, that had been found as the barge was being unloaded. Mr. Goll leaned over, parted some hessian and exposed a man's body. In an awkward attempt to lighten the gravity of the situation, Goll remarked, "I can safely assume, Sir, that you did not make an order for this addition to the cargo." Scrooge was not tempted to levity, but he did recognize the man's sincerity, and could certainly appreciate it. Until, that is, he looked upon the corpse.

Of a sudden, all of the air in Scrooge's lungs was involuntarily expelled and it took several seconds before he could issue any reaction. Once he was able to breathe again, the unbidden sound that came from his throat could only be described as a desperate cry of pain. It was evidence of Scrooge's unexpected recognition of the human remains, and it brought with it shock and unutterable, intolerable loss, for Scrooge had found himself staring at the lifeless face of his nephew, Fred.

Scrooge stumbled backward, helpless and unable to see or think, and it took the strength of both Homer and the constable to prevent him from caving into a heap onto the ground. They propped him up until he could sit on a nearby stack of cargo, then both men returned to the barge, anxious to know what could possibly have brought on this sort of reaction. At the sight of the corpse, Homer gasped loudly in disbelief, and stood immobile. Rollo's reaction, however, was laced with curses. The man had no doubt been dead for some days, yet his identity was unquestionable.

With haste, Homer returned to Scrooge to offer support while Norris, being used to this sort of thing, as well as being responsible for the inquiry, immediately took the lead in the examination. It was always more difficult to play the Peeler over the decease of a friendly acquaintance, but the constable quickly got to work, nevertheless.

It was impossible to know precisely how long the man had been dead, but his flesh was beginning to decompose. Norris also noticed that his face was unshaven, and he was not wearing one of the well-tailored suits for which Fred was generally known. He was, instead, outfitted cheaply. The clothing may have had a degree of quality at one time, but it was long worn and somewhat tattered. Still, the body definitely resembled Mr. Symons — that could not be denied — and both Scrooge and Homer certainly knew him well enough to be positive about his identity. No, there was no way around it, and Norris's wishing it were not so would not change things. They were, indeed, dealing with the remains of Fred Symons.

Norris turned the body over and could find no apparent marks of violence. Although such an assumption would require verification by a surgeon, the initial evidence indicated that the man had most likely not been murdered. Norris was not generally moved by dealing with the dead, but he knew this man, or rather, had known him in life, and had genuinely liked and respected him. It made his assignment more difficult, but it also filled him with a determination that was fueled by outrage.

Addressing the wharfinger, Norris asked, "Who is the owner of this barge, and where is he?" Pointing toward a passage, Mr. Goll replied, "He went to the Abandoned Maiden, an inn just down that way and 'round the corner to the right. Says he needs to get back up north quick-like, to pick up another cargo, but I told him he wasn't going anywhere soon, least ways not until you Peelers tell him he can. If this is the sort of cargo he's used to carrying, it's likely he won't be doing much business in future, other than counting the hours in Newgate!" Then he recalled, "Actually, there's two of 'em. One owns the craft and the other is his boatman. They aren't like many of the boaters who are clean and steady. These two are cut a bit rough. They both could use a talking-to, if you ask me."

Norris hadn't asked him, but he appreciated the information all the same, and planned to do exactly that – the sooner the better – but first, he must see to Scrooge.

Scrooge was no longer slumping heavily on the pile of cargo. He now stood erect and stable as a warrior facing battle. He had initially been in no shape to assist but had quickly recovered and was now able to think clearly. His many years of dealing with the ups and downs of business had prepared him for bad luck, and even though nothing could compare with the "bad luck" of this day, he was able to resort to his established habits and begin to apply clear thinking to the situation. He was no weakling, either in body or character, and there was no way under Heaven that the constable would pursue this matter without him! His desire to be involved was, like Norris's, fueled by an unquenchable fury. He would see this thing through – or die in the attempt. He owed Fred that much.

Having sent Homer back to the counting-house with the admonition that he relate the matter to no one but Cratchit, Scrooge and Norris set off for the Abandoned Maiden to begin their search for the truth, and to affect justice for Fred. Both were silent on the short walk to the inn, each lost in his own thoughts. One, a loving Uncle facing the intolerable death of a beloved nephew who was more like a son; the other, a Peeler who cared about the victim, but also had a case to solve.

CB&CO

Homer was in no hurry to return to the counting-house. He was going to have to give the tragic news to Cratchit and he had no idea what he should say, or how to say it, but the task was his to perform. It must be done, and it must be done now. Still, he took his time. He directed the cabby to put him out at a distance from the office, from where he proceeded on foot at a plod. It did no good. He was no more composed when he arrived than when he had left the Basin. In fact, being back at the office of Scrooge and Symons made it a great deal worse.

"Is that you, Homer?", called Cratchit as Homer passed through the door and slowly closed it. Homer gave an affirmative grunt and removed his hat, hanging it on the rack near the entry. The office was cozy and at any other time he would have been pleased to return to its comforts, but not today – not now. He managed to reply, "Yes, Mr. Cratchit. It is I, and we must talk."

Cratchit caught the inflection in Homer's voice and stood down from his stool, to greet him as he came further into the office. One look at Homer's countenance told him something was terribly amiss.

Alarmed, he cried, "What is it, my boy? What's happened, and where is Mr. Scrooge?"

Without intending to be rude by sitting in the presence of his superior, Homer was suddenly overcome, and sank into a nearby chair, putting his head in his hands. Cratchit was imagining all sorts of things when Homer eventually managed to say, "It's Mr. Symons. Oh, dear God in Heaven, it's Mr. Fred," before he burst into tears, not minding about the unmanliness of crying, nor of doing so in front of another man.

"Mr. Symons?", asked Cratchit, his eyes wide in disbelief. Homer did not respond right away and Cratchit was ready to grab him by the shoulders and shake him. "What about him? Tell me! I must know, although I gather it is the worst of news."

Homer gulped, staunching the tears. "He was on the boat. I mean, his body was wrapped up and stowed in the barge we brokered!" Homer blew his nose in his handkerchief, settled somewhat, and said, more clearly this time, "He was packed in among the paper and leather and transported to London from somewhere in the north. We don't know anything yet, other than he's dead, but at least it doesn't appear that he died violently." He looked at Cratchit, searching for any answer the elder man could give, and insisted, "I thought he was in Holland! Wasn't he to be in the Netherlands, or even Belgium or Denmark?"

"Yes, Lad, he was." Cratchit walked several feet, turned back to face Homer, and repeated, "Dead! This can't be. There must be some mistake. Are you absolutely certain?"

Nodding, Homer answered, "Yessir, I am. Mr. Scrooge nearly collapsed when he saw him, then Norris and I took a look, and it was Mr. Symons, alright. We all knew who it was." He shut his eyes, but quickly opened them rather than revisit the sight of that lifeless face. Then he remembered what else he was to tell Cratchit.

"Mr. Cratchit, Mr. Scrooge says we're not to tell anyone else about this. No one. Do you agree?"

Cratchit agreed, and once he had been sworn to secrecy he and Homer spent some time sitting together, shaking their heads over the unbelievable occurrence, recalling Fred Symons and admitting they had no idea what this terrible, senseless death could mean.

ᘓᘔ

Within minutes of leaving the dock, Scrooge and Norris arrived at the Abandoned Maiden Inn, which befitted its name. It felt forsaken and alone, unfit for pleasant company. The name on the shingle had faded with time and the sign appeared to be hanging by a thread of rope. It was definitely uninviting, and neither wanted to enter, but they must.

As the two men crossed the threshold, their eyes were almost useless. Very little sunlight was allowed to creep in through small glass panes, but what dim light there was hosted blankets of dust motes as they floated freely throughout. The interior was dingy and unkempt, and odors of stale tobacco and dirty bodies made a hostile assault on the nostrils. A creaky staircase stood near the dilapidated fireplace, where a few embers of coal had once warmed nothing but a small portion of itself. Close to the fireplace sat two men on wooden benches. A wobbly table was between them, into which decades of etchings had been carved, and each man held a tankard of watered-down ale. Since there was no one else in the place, Scrooge and Norris rightly assumed they were the boaters.

Scrooge and Norris approached the table and the older man stood, to assert himself, and addressed Norris. "I know what you're after, and we ain't done nuthin'. We was as surprised as anyone to see that corpse lyin' in th' barge, all trussed up and 'idden away, so don' go gittin' ideas about pinnin' this on us." It wasn't his intention, but his voice suddenly took on a whiny tone. "Look 'ere, somebody's used us ill to get rid of a body, 'n that's the truth of the matter, so don' be cookin' up fancy tales, to make it look like we done somthin' wrong."

"Are you the owner of the barge?", asked Norris, his tone indicating he would tolerate no nonsense.

"I am. I'm Duff, the skipper, an' this 'ere's Wigley, my boatman. We jus' come down from Aylesbury. So's you know, I run a 'onest business, takin' cargo from 'ere to there. I don' go about transportin' dead people. Leastwise, I never 'ave, but that's not to say I wouldn't do it 'onest-like, if I was hired to do it by 'onest people, for 'onest reasons."

"I've not accused you of anything," replied Norris. "I simply need to find out what you know, in order to discover how the man ended up on your barge, and to learn the facts of his decease." He noticed that Wigley refused to look up, as if to avoid running the risk of being asked a question. He was keeping his eyes on his knuckles, which were white from gripping his tankard.

Duff continued. "I don' know nuthin' 'bout any of what you said, 'n neither does Wigley. 'E don' know any more'n I do. All we was doin' was carryin' a load of leather 'n paper from Aylesbury to London, an' we didn't see the body 'til they checked it when we got 'ere. Look — we're plain folk, an' it appears we're just stupid enough to be used for foul purposes. I admit I ain't 'appy about all this, but I don' know 'ow or why it 'append, an' I don' know 'ow to 'elp. I would, if I could. We just wanna get back on the canal soon's the barge's unloaded and we're free t' go."

"I don't know when that may be," replied Norris, "but you will remain here tonight, at the least. First, however, I need to know where you took on the load, and all of the stops you made on your way here"

Wondering why he need repeat himself, Duff pursed his lips, inhaled deeply, and blew the air through his nose, to show his frustration. "Like I already tol' ya, we took on the cargo at Aylesbury — I think it come from Chesham — an' then we 'eaded down the Grand Junction Canal. We come through several locks 'n put by in a couple o' places, but there wasn't nuthin' out of the ordinary that 'append. No extra passengers 'n no more cargo, 'ceptin' this 'ere corpse, that is, but we didn't know 'e were there! An' b'fore you ask, we was there when the cargo went on the boat, so the body weren't there when we set out!"

"And just when do you reckon the body may have been placed in the barge?", asked Norris.

"Th' only times would'a been when we ducked into a local tavern, quick-like. If someone were watchin' fer a boat they'd a' seen us go, an' used our absence to do their dirty work," replied Duff, insisting that he could not recall exactly which taverns they may have entered. It was a route they often took, so it was impossible to distinguish one trip from another.

There seemed little more they could ask, so Norris and Scrooge both turned to go, but not before Scrooge glared at both men and said, simply, "You had best be innocent of anything to do with this man's death or his mishandling afterward because, if you are culpable to any degree, I will not only pursue punishment by all the law allows, I will also find a way to impose my own personal punishment, and that is a promise." His threat was based on his love for Fred, but it also sounded like the "old" Scrooge — the one whose conscience was seared — the one who knew how to get things done regardless of the cost to anyone involved. Both boaters instinctively believed he had the means and the will to follow through. What was raw grief for Scrooge displayed itself to the boaters as a willingness to wield malevolent power, and to destroy anyone, or anything, that might hinder him.

Once outside, Scrooge and Norris discussed things further. Both had seen Wigley's refusal to look at them, and both had sensed the fear he was trying to hide. He knew something, but it appeared that Duff was unaware of it. It was clear they might not get much from the boaters, but they knew who they were and how to find them, for the time being.

Norris could lie in wait, to see who might attempt to retrieve the body, but it was no doubt too late for that. If someone were watching for this particular body they would surely know it had been discovered and was in the hands of the Peelers. They may even have intended to retrieve the body at an earlier junction, and failed. Had Fred's body been removed from the barge at some point on the canal, no one would have been the wiser and Fred's disappearance would have remained a mystery forever. Having looked upon his nephew's deteriorating face, Scrooge wasn't sure which would have been the easier to bear; never knowing, or seeing him in his present state.

Scrooge and Norris took a cab from the Basin and it was at a corner not far from his house that Scrooge disembarked. "If you please, Constable," said Scrooge, "I will retreat to my home now. I'm overcome by these events and must also speak with Catherine anon, but now I need only myself for company." Rather than try to say something meaningful, Norris simply nodded, and they said their good-byes with the understanding that they would meet on the morrow at 1:00 o'clock. As Scrooge strode away, his back to Norris, his brave, stiffly upright bearing could not prevent the tears that streamed down his face.

After parting from Scrooge, Norris stopped at the counting-house to ensure that Cratchit knew of the matter and that he would keep it to himself. He could add little to what Homer had already told Cratchit, other than that the boaters were not helpful. Norris and Homer spent several moments exchanging bits of information, none of it new.

As the two men spoke, Cratchit noted that their mutual concern for Scrooge and their admiration of Fred Symons, as well as having shared the moment of discovering his body, fostered a truce of some sort between them. Cratchit also knew it mightn't last forever, since they both cared a great deal for his daughter Martha, and the rivalry was of the most basic sort — competition for the prize. Still, he did hope it might at least ease a bit of the enmity between them.

As he thought on it, Cratchit admitted to himself that he wasn't so much concerned with the well-being of these men. It was with Martha he was lately troubled. She was such a good lass, and true of heart, but her beauty and her poise did draw attention from many who would gladly court her and love her, if only they had the opportunity. Thus far she had not realized her power over men, and he hoped she never would. He did not want her to lose her lovely innocence, nor did he want her heart to be damaged. He could not guarantee his reaction to anyone who would mistreat her. For those reasons he kept a watchful eye on both Homer Probert and Rollo Norris. He had a preference between the two, but had not yet admitted it, even to himself.

CHAPTER EIGHT

Catherine

A s far as Scrooge was concerned, that night was the darkest night of his life. Oh, he had endured fear, disappointments and decline during his lifetime, even since his character had been renewed, but this was like being buried alive. He thought back to the visitation of the Spirit of Christmas-Yet-to-Come on Christmas Eve of 1843, and recalled the sight of that horrible tombstone with his name etched into it so definitively. The idea of dying alone and unloved, leaving a legacy worth only forgetting, had finally turned him around. Tonight, however, he felt as if he were actually in that grave after all, and he was finding it difficult to breathe in such a deep, dark place of no escape. This time there really was no way out. His life was over and any fine and virtuous legacy he might have had, had died with Fred.

Why would this happen? This not only makes no sense, it is beyond the pale. When Fan died I lost the one person in the world who loved me, and now I have lost her son, my precious nephew. There is no rational explanation for it. None. Could he have died of natural causes? Who would kill Fred, and why? How? Where?

Scrooge should have known what would next occur, but he was so lost in his intolerable grief and unanswerable thoughts that he was taken by surprise when he heard the familiar, "Scrooooooge."

Oh, no! Not Marley. Not now. I don't need a lecture. I just need to weep, and I need to do so alone. Marley, old partner, please float back through that wall, and leave me be.

Nevertheless, he was hailed by a repeated, "Scrooooooge!" He had learnt on that first Christmas Eve, and several times since, that when Marley's image wanted to speak with him it was no good plugging his ears, covering his eyes, or trying to reason him away. He had once tried burying his head under his bed covers, but it hadn't deterred Marley in the least. So, for what felt like the hundredth time in an eighteen-month, Scrooge readied himself for whatever was to follow.

"My old friend," said Marley, in a surprisingly sympathetic voice, "things are not always what they seem. What mortals often consider to be the worst possible occurrences can have surprising and rewarding outcomes. This occurrence is not providential, but I remind you of what the Rector told you some months ago about the Biblical meaning of your name. He said it was 'Hitherto hath the Lord helped us.' It's as the Rector said – that help was not just for the past. It is also for your future, for you do have one."

Scrooge wanted to laugh in Marley's indistinct face, but he was too miserable to manage anything other than a wry twist of his top lip.

"Future? You tell me I have a future at what is, for all intents and purposes, the end of my life, as well as my nephew's? What good can possibly come from this evil situation?"

Ever persistent, Marley replied, "Do not over-examine, my friend. Do not over-examine," and with that, Marley's form, such as it was, faded until he was no more. It was only after his disappearance that Scrooge recalled the questions he planned to ask Marley about Mr. Carter, but it was no matter. Nothing much seemed to matter, and Marley had certainly not been of any real assistance.

Scrooge had often been wearied by Marley's riddles without answers, which were followed by his abrupt departures that left Scrooge without a solution, and Marley had done it again. Do not 'over-examine?' *Alright, old friend, I will try to proceed without giving thought to the pain within my breast, but I challenge you to help me find the words when I have to tell Catherine what has become of her husband!* Scrooge admitted to himself that, although Marley had been a fairly easy companion in life, in death he could be downright impossible!

CB&O

The next morning found Scrooge on the Symons doorstep, wishing he were anywhere else. Other than the few who were originally privy to the situation, no one was yet aware of what had occurred, and Norris had managed to keep it from the newspapers. Scrooge was determined to inform Catherine himself, rather than chance her hearing it from a servant or anyone who was not family. She had no close relations other than her younger sister, Flora, who would have had a difficult time telling Catherine anything untoward, much less the death of her husband, and it would not be fair to saddle Flora with that task.

Scrooge hesitated before using the knocker, but eventually managed to rap on the door. His heart was pounding furiously as a maid with a very bright smile led him to the morning room. He had taken this route many times, but today the name had a double meaning for Scrooge, for it was about to become the "mourning" room. Catherine was now a widow, and he was the one who must tell her so. It was the most heart-rending thing he had ever been charged to do.

Catherine sat in her chair, looking radiant. He had never seen her look more beautiful and he knew, of a sudden, that she was much more than he realized, although he had always thought very highly of her. He could see, even more, why Fred had fallen so deeply in love with her. Catherine was not only lovely, she was the epitome of what a young woman should be. Never mind that she could be somewhat headstrong when she wanted her way, such as the time she insisted that Scrooge learn the latest dance steps, and absolutely would not accept his refusal to cooperate. In that instance her efforts had proven fortuitous because Scrooge had enjoyed himself immensely, and could now partner any lady for any dance, without shaming himself, or her.

Scrooge and Catherine greeted each the other before Scrooge took his usual place on a love seat across from her. He eschewed the emptiness of Fred's chair and closed his eyes for a moment, finding courage.

"Catherine, I fear I am here on a dark errand and it will do neither of us any good to put off the news I must break to you. You must steady yourself, My Dear." Her eyes darkened as she knew the news must, of course, concern her husband, and she stiffened as she sensed it was a dire report.

"But of course, Uncle." Jutting her chin, she said, "You needn't coddle me. I am a grown woman, and although I am very afraid of what you are about to say, please be quickly done with it. It is about Fred, is it not? Is he in danger? Is he injured — or worse? Please, just tell me."

Scrooge swallowed hard, leaned forward and took both her hands in his, trying to be gentle, but holding her fingers just a bit too tightly. "My Dear . . . Fred is gone from us." She stared, opened her mouth to speak, hesitated, then whispered, "Gone? Truly gone? Are you quite certain?"

"Yes, Dear One. I verified with my own eyes the fact that he is dead." There, he had said it, but he would have given his entire fortune not to have had to. He knew the words made a wound that would never heal. He had also introduced the terrible void that would now occupy her existence forever, but there was no way around it. "I can tell you what details I know," said Scrooge, "but they are few." He was the messenger of horrific tidings and he was weighed down with guilt for giving her injury, but he must continue.

"Although we do not yet know the cause, it seems he died somewhere in the north, while we all believed him to be in the Netherlands." He asked if she knew any reason why Fred might have returned to England and was not surprised that she knew nothing.

Scrooge might as well tell her what few facts remained. "There is something else I do not understand, and that is his attire. Fred was dressed in near rags. I doubt he even owns clothing that old. It was also fairly dirty, and you and I both know he is . . . was . . . very particular about his toilette." Still silent, she nodded her agreement, then asked, "But Uncle, this makes no sense. How did you discover these things?"

"His body was found in a barge that I brokered, so I was contacted. I did not know I would be dealing with a body, much less that of my beloved nephew, but that is all I can tell you." She was searching his face for something, anything that might give a bit of hope and suggest less finality, but when he had nothing more to offer, her eyes filled with tears. He said, simply, "Yes, Catherine, we are now alone."

Letting go of his hands, Catherine rose and sat next to him on the loveseat, her lower lip quivering as she began to speak. "No, Uncle. We are not alone, neither of us, as long as we have each other, and of course there is my sister Flora, who is so dear and can always be relied upon." Here she hesitated, dabbing her eyes and nose with a handkerchief before sitting up straight and announcing in a less than confident voice, "And soon there will be another. For you see, I need you now even more than ever, because, in a few months I'm going to have a child. An autumn child, I am told, which will mean he or she will be here in time to increase the delight of Christmas." Scrooge was unprepared for the information and was reeling between grief and joy. He couldn't believe what he was hearing! So that was why Catherine was radiant. His thoughts raced as she continued.

"Fred and I so wanted to make it a grand announcement when we told you. We had planned a dinner party with you and a few who are close to us . . ." Her voice broke on the last few words, and with that she dropped her head on his breast, clung to him and sobbed as if her very heart would break.

When she could again speak, Catherine sat up and said, "You are aware that Flora and I lost our father when we were very young, and we have been motherless for years. I am wondering . . . do you think your friend Mrs. Langstone would be willing to be my friend, too?" Wiping her eyes, she said, "Oh, I have enough acquaintances, but they are as fickle and capricious as I, and at a time like this a woman needs parents." She smiled at him with open admiration, and explained.

"I have you, but I believe I need a woman too, who is older and wiser than I. You know how often Fred accused me of being a little less than practical, and a woman who is about to become a mother needs to know what to do. Fred would insist upon it." She attempted a small, brave smile that made them both weep again over the loss they could not contain. They sat for some time, clinging to each other and hoping that sharing their pain could somehow divide it by half.

Finally, Scrooge spoke. "Now, My Dear, I know this may be too much for you take in at this time, but I must at least tell you that you will be well provided for, you and the child. Fred saw to that soon after I made him my partner and I will continue to manage your affairs to ensure that you are never in want of anything." He had delivered the worst possible news and had been given the best of news. *Marley, why could you not have simply told me? A child! A grand-nephew or niece, who will be like a grandchild to me!* In no way did it lessen the loss, but it did bring the merest speck of hope – something to look forward to. Fred would, through his child, live on.

CHAPTER NINE

The Abandoned Maiden

Scrooge and Norris met at the George and Vulture early that afternoon, to decide how to proceed with the boaters before Norris released them and their barge. Neither of them was able to be absolutely fair-minded because both were driven by the intensity of their sentiments.

The two men discussed the impending meeting over a luncheon of meat pies, but they did not enjoy their food. They were too anxious to be at the Abandoned Maiden, to collect whatever information the boaters could tell them. They bolted their meals quickly and set out.

Norris was in charge of the investigation, but he also knew Scrooge, and could foresee that Scrooge would not hesitate to insert himself into any conversation or activity if he were feeling short-tempered. Norris decided to warn him away from turning this meeting into a mix-up, since he was convinced he had greater self-control than Scrooge, particularly since he was not a relation of the victim. Norris feared that Scrooge's grief could bring on a physical altercation, which had been known to have the opposite effect when attempting to elicit information. He suspected that Scrooge was determined to squeeze every last bit of information from the boaters, regardless of the pain it might cause, and he could almost read Scrooge's mind as they neared the inn. He rightly discerned that Scrooge was thinking, *we need information, and hang the methods it might require!* Norris hoped he could keep Scrooge tightly tethered by issuing a well-stated, yet polite, warning. At the least, he could make the attempt.

"Mr. Scrooge, I realize you are extremely anxious to bear down on these men, and I am of the same mind, but I ask that you allow me to play the lead since I am the constable. Perhaps that rank of authority will assist us in obtaining some useful facts from them in the shortest amount of time. I am fairly certain we will not be forced to resort to physical tactics."

Scrooge readily agreed, although Norris was unconvinced. He would keep a watchful eye on the gentleman and put a stop to any violent outbursts that might cause Scrooge embarrassment or jeopardize the investigation.

Upon their arrival at the Abandoned Maiden, the Constable and Scrooge glanced over the several patrons within and located the boaters in the same spot they had left them the day before. They had not changed their expressions, and each had another diluted ale before him. Neither looked anxious to talk, but Norris and Scrooge stood over them, emphasizing their authority. Norris began.

"I would say 'Good afternoon' to you men, if it were one, but it is not since this gentleman here has suffered the loss of his nephew and heir, and you have played a role in what may have been a murder." Both boaters shifted slightly on their benches but did not look up. They would be mulish, no matter what. Norris was betting that they were afraid, for all of their play-acting, so he pushed on, hoping to use to that fear to his advantage.

"Duff, you own the barge and that places you right in the middle of this crime. It is your boat that transported the body, and that is a fact. I would say that leaves you in the position of having to prove you either knew nothing about it (he noticed Duff's side glance to Wigley), or you had a legal reason for doing so, which I doubt." He decided it was time to apply more pressure and he asked, "What do you have to say for yourself? Have you any defense that will keep me from placing you under arrest right now?" That did the trick.

Duff jumped up and cried, "I didn't do nothin' wrong! I told you b'fore, I run a 'onest game and I didn't know nothin' 'bout no body in me boat!" He had heard enough and was not going to pay the price for something he did not do. With that, he glared straight at Wigley, pointed his index finger close to his face and demanded, "Tell 'em! You tell 'em what you jus' tol' me. Do it!"

The exchange jolted the atmosphere of the inn and the anticipation of reaching some truth of this matter spurred Norris on. Scrooge was managing to stand still and merely observe, but he did not miss a single syllable that was spoken. His hands were balled into fists and his jaw was working.

Norris turned to Wigley and said, in a very low voice, "Yes, tell us. It may mean at least deportation if you do, but it will more likely mean your neck if you don't, because I will pin anything and everything on you that I can manage to prove." His voice rose in volume as he added, "And I swear I won't care if it's true or not, so you'd best begin speaking — now!"

Wigley sat still and crossed his arms in defiance. He had decided he would not be brow-beaten into saying anything, but he had not reckoned on the temper he may encounter. Arms still crossed, he glared up at Norris and growled, "I ain't got nuthin' to say – not to you nor that fancy toff standin' there 'oo thinks 'e's lost so much. 'E still has more'n I'll ever 'ave, with all his losin'.'"

Scrooge minded his promise to Norris and kept himself in check, but Norris sprang on the man. He was enraged and needed something to strike, and the desire to beat this man into compliance overrode his ability to contain himself. Grabbing Wigley by the collar, he yanked him up and struck him with his fists until he fell back against the fireplace, slid down to the filthy floor and swiped his cut lip with a frayed sleeve. Realizing what had just occurred, he jumped up and went for Norris.

Like dogs at a bear-baiting, the few patrons in the place perked their ears and caught the scent of blood. They would not stand by while one of their own was knocked about. Within the time it took to cross the room, two of them landed on Norris and two on Scrooge, while the others stood by and yelled encouragement to their mates, although they had no idea why. Regardless, they heartily approved of what they considered just desserts for the privileged class.

Both Scrooge and Norris were tall men, and unafraid of a skirmish, although Scrooge's last fracas in his own counting house had resulted in a dismal defeat. Recalling that failure set him to defending himself in a most efficacious manner. He rammed his elbow into the stomach of the man who had him by the throat from behind, knocking the wind out of him, and left him rolling on the floor. He then went after his remaining attacker like a windmill in a high gale. His flailing arms were too much for the man because it was impossible to make out how and when the next blow was coming. So, he backed away, giving up the fight that was never his. Scrooge pulled one of the attackers from Norris and sent him flying far enough that he opted not to rejoin the fray. Both Scrooge and Norris were then able to contend with the remaining patron, as well as Wigley, who was near to surrendering, at any rate.

Unfortunately, the commotion had also attracted attention from the street, and three more men entered the inn to join the melee, not knowing, or caring, what the fight represented. They simply jumped on those closest to them, who happened to be the two patrons who had been bested by Scrooge, and Skipper Duff, and began their own fisticuffs. The barkeep, a large man who had no concern for anything other than his establishment, rescued Duff, then aided Scrooge in pulling his remaining patron from Norris. By then Wigley had, once again, slumped to the floor, leaving Norris free to shout to everyone that he was a Peeler, and to cease the rumpus immediately.

The rest of the tavern's patrons and the men from the street were now exchanging blows, and no one heeded Norris's warning, nor were they at all concerned with who he was. They would not stop until they had fought long enough to satisfy their need for brutal exhilaration. When they at last grew tired and had garnered enough cuts and bruises to satisfy them for at least a week, the inn finally quietened. Their energy was spent, and they did not argue when Norris emptied the place, chasing everyone out excepting the boaters and the proprietor, who moved off to straighten the rubble.

The inn had survived without much damage, other than a broken chair and a few scattered tankards. A good amount of ale had been spilt which, when wiped up, may have been the nearest thing to a mopping the floor had seen in ages. The inn had, in fact, done better than the boaters, who were bloodied and tattered, particularly Wigley. Norris and Scrooge were somewhat disheveled, but a few tugs at their clothing and a run of the fingers through their hair made them presentable, other than some bruising on Norris's face and a few scrapes on their knuckles. The boaters limped back to the benches, somewhat dispirited, and Norris began where he had left off, almost as if there had been no interruption. Scrooge maintained his stance as observer, wryly recalling Norris's warning to him to mind his temper.

The one good result of the brawl was Wigley's being convinced that Norris would brook no stubborn silence, and that he meant what he said. It had been enough to convince the boater to tell what he knew, after a fashion, so when Norris said, "I will ask you once again, and one time only, what you know about the body," the man began to talk, but on his own terms.

"First off, I ain't sayin' that I done nothin' wrong, but I could see you was lookin' to put the blame on someone — any poor sod would do for you — so I kept me mouth shut. Still 'n all, I can give you a fanciful story, if you jus' need to 'ear sumthin." He had begun like a barrister before the bench and Scrooge realized the man was no fool. He could think clearly and most likely vindicate himself, at least to himself, for any act that would enrich him by a few coins. Wigley continued, revealing his own thoughts on why the body may have been placed in the barge, even though he presented it as if the entire thing were a fairy tale.

"Ev'rbody's 'eard about this 'ere Anatomy Act, 'n how them surgeons 'ave enough bodies to tear into these days. Still, there is the odd body what's sent to some out-o'-the way surgeon, what don't come strictly within the letter o' the law, for some reason." After pinching his bloodied nose, he continued.

"Now, I ain't sayin' as I would ever do such a thing, but let's say, imaginary like, that I was to agree t' look th' other way while some bloke planted a maybe not-so-legal cadaver in the boat. 'Ow would I know what's a legal body 'n what ain't? 'An' 'ow would I know if it was even intended for cuttin' up? Wot would be the 'arm, I ask you? Th' poor creature's lived 'is life, died and gone on to 'is rightful reward — or deserved punishment — so the part of 'im what's real ain't around no longer. All's left is that part what can't go no further. It's like throwaway, right?" He gingerly pressed his bruised cheekbone and continued in an effort to justify himself.

"'Sides," he decided to add, "It ain't particurly agin' the law no more for some bodies to be used for cuttin' up, so, as I see it, th' only thing I might'a done wrong (if I was to 'ave done anythin' at all) would be the not knowin' for sure where this partic'lar body come from, 'n not particurly carin', for that matter." He coughed and spat out a tooth that had been loosed in the fight. He wasn't finished with justifying his actions.

"As far as all this cuttin' up 'n sendin' dead bodies 'ere 'n there, say some poor surgeon way down in Lonnon knows his patient's got an 'eart, 'n lungs, 'n stomach 'n such, but 'e ain't never seen 'em. Then, when it comes time to open 'im up and fix things, 'e don't know 'ow to do it 'cause 'e ain't never 'ad a look inside b'fore. 'E needs to know what's in there, don't 'e? If 'e gets the chance to look inside some poor bloke's used-up body 'n learns 'ow to fiddle around in there, won't 'e be a fitter surgeon? 'Ow's anybody gonna get 'urt in such a situation? An' if the one 'oo's sendin' 'im the body wants to slip me (imaginary-like, you unnerstand) a quid to let 'im 'elp out 'is fellow man, where's the 'arm, I ask you? If a dead man's scraps can save a live man's body, I don't see as 'ow the Almighty would exactly frown on it. The way I unnerstand it, once a fellow dies, the Almighty ain't got no further use for his flesh, right?"

Scrooge was hard-put to come up with a reply of any sort, although he didn't approve of anything that was unlawful, and dissecting Fred's body was absolutely illegal since he was not from a poorhouse or prison.

In addition, his family had definitely not given permission for dissection. Still, this working man's logic was a thought-out argument. Either that, or he had a very quick wit. Scrooge felt no compassion for Wigley, who was nothing less than a criminal accomplice to a possible murder. Scrooge could never bring himself to countenance Fred's body being used in such a way, and he sympathized with those families who felt forced to do so due to their inability to pay for burial.

Scrooge glanced at Norris, who's expression mirrored his own. If the body were intended for dissection, Norris could arrest Wigley for breaking the Queen's law, since it could easily be proven that the body did not come within the provisions of the Anatomy Act. It might be more difficult to prove that transporting the corpse had constituted a criminal act, since Wigley would no doubt deny knowing the body was there. In addition, Norris could only imagine the effect Wigley's philosophical arguments might have on a jury. In a court of law, it was often Norris's trained experience against an unschooled thinker, but in this case, he wouldn't wager on the outcome. Knowing that the possibility of reformation was unlikely, Norris nevertheless admonished Wigley, aware that his warning washed over the boater like a gentle, refreshing breeze.

As they were leaving the poor Abandoned Maiden, Scrooge turned back and asked Wigley, "In your imaginary scheme of things, had a body, say, been loaded into your barge, where do you imagine that might have taken place? And would you know the identity of whoever made the transaction, or who placed the body in the barge?"

"Well, now," drawled Wigley as he ran his finger around the rim of his tankard, "If I was to conjure up a little more to the tale, I would most likely imagine that th' body would'a been laid in the barge near the Marsworth Locks. I wouldn't'a known 'oo the bloke was though, would I, since it would'a occurred when me back was turned at th' local pub, 'n any 'rangements would'a been made through a tyke I'd never seen b'fore. That's if it 'ad ever really 'append, that is."

"And just how were you planning to explain the body, once you arrived in London?", pressed Norris.

Wigley was untroubled by the question. "There wouldn't be no 'splainin' to do, would there, if we din't know 'ow the body got there. We'd be victims too, wouldn't we? Matter o' fact, I s'pose that's zackly what we are! We're victims!"

The man was disgraceful, and Scrooge was more than pleased that Norris had given him a thrashing. He deserved it, and Norris had certainly earned the pleasure. Scrooge's only regret was that he had allowed Norris to warn him away from pummeling the man, himself!

Scrooge and Norris walked back, re-examining this morning's occurrences. So, this mightn't be simply a matter of someone's wanting to get rid of Fred's body. No, it might be worse, if anything could be. Wigley's assumptions regarding the body could be correct. It might actually be possible that Fred's body was intended to be dissected! Norris's initial inspection of the body at the canal dock had not indicated he was murdered, and although he wanted the boaters to fear they might be involved in a murder, the fact was that the barge may have been simply a means of disposal, or delivery. His body was perhaps being sent to a medical novice who was not in a position to obtain a body legally, who would slice him open then toss his remains aside, all the while calling it science. Worse, Scrooge had heard tell of bodies being dismembered, the body parts then distributed for dissection, which would place them outside the rules of the Anatomy Act. Well, Scrooge supposed it really was science, but the idea sickened him until, at one point, he was forced to run into an alley and empty the contents of his stomach. It was as if he were trying to rid himself of the ugliness of the matter, but he was not at all successful.

Scrooge did not discuss it with Norris at the time, but he had made up his mind to pursue this thing to its end, wherever and whatever that might be. He would begin by instructing Homer to use Fred's itinerary and send dispatches to each individual, or group, with whom Fred was to meet. Scrooge would then know who Fred had seen, and where he had failed to appear. It was Scrooge's intent to travel to the last place where Fred had been seen, and do his own detecting. He must take care of a few things in London first, such as assisting Catherine and burying Fred, but then he would be free to travel, and he was determined to discover what had happened to his nephew.

CHAPTER TEN

Edwin Carter Consults Bob Cratchit

The following day the ever-faithful Bob Cratchit was alone in the counting-house, deep in thought. Since the loss of Fred, Cratchit was recounting his years with the people who had occupied this space. He had first been in the employ of Scrooge and Marley and, although it had often been a difficult situation, he had many memories that, for some reason, were intent on imposing themselves on him at this moment.

Unlike Scrooge, Mr. Marley had been a contradiction in character. Whereas Scrooge had been a miserable miser and no mistake, Marley was a composite of traits. He was not entirely in want of a sympathetic heart and a few of his acquaintances had somehow suspected that. Wasn't it Marley to whom Scrooge's sister Fan had written when she was in need of advice? Wasn't it Marley who granted Mr. Carter a loan for his start in the New World, for whatever the reason? Didn't Marley leave his home to Scrooge, who now resided therein? Yes, Marley and Scrooge had been similar in general behavior, and both were known in business circles as the most shrewd and heartless men in London, but Marley seemed, at least to Cratchit, to be just a bit more of a humanitarian in those days. He had been different somehow, and Cratchit always found him to be an interesting character, even though he had never been at ease in Marley's presence.

As he contemplated these things, Cratchit absentmindedly wandered into Marley's old office which Fred, of late, had occupied. He ran his hand over the worn surface of the heavy wood desk, something he would not have considered doing while Jacob Marley was nearby. In those days Cratchit had been only too well aware that one false step could result in being severely admonished, receiving a cut in salary, or losing his situation altogether. No, it could not be denied that there had been real improvements in the people and practices in the past two years. Yet, and although Cratchit admired and respected Fred very much, he must admit that there were those odd times when he almost missed having Old Marley about. Almost.

While lost in his reverie, Cratchit heard someone enter the front office and scurried to greet whomever it might be. He was pleased when it turned out to be Edwin Carter who, since his return from America, was now managing his business endeavors through this office. He was always amiable, but today he was not his usual self. He was not as jovial. In fact, he appeared to be preoccupied and somewhat downcast. Without his usual smile, Mr. Carter said, "Ah, Mr. Cratchit. I see I have caught you alone and I apologize if I am taking you away from anything pressing, but I do need to look over some of the contracts you are preparing for our new venture. I promise not to interfere with your other duties." He frowned and added, "I did, also, wish to offer everyone my condolences on the wickedness that befell Mr. Symons. I only knew him briefly, but I was very taken with him. I know this is a terrible loss to you all, particularly Mr. Scrooge."

It did not worry Cratchit to cease his work for a few minutes. He was fastidious in his endeavors and was, therefore, invariably ahead in his tasks, so he could afford to step down from his station for a bit. In addition, it appeared that Mr. Carter was in need of some pleasant conversation.

"Thank you for your sympathy, Mr. Carter. It is most appreciated, and it is no bother to show you the documents as they stand. I would, in fact, be glad of the company." The men sat, and Cratchit made tea from the pot of hot water on the hob, then they quickly reviewed the proposed contracts. Once they had done so, Mr. Carter leaned back in his chair, crossed his legs and heaved a great sigh. He didn't speak, nor did he seem anxious to be leaving.

"I don't want to be impertinent," ventured Cratchit, "but is there something weighing on you, Mr. Carter?"

Without hesitation Carter replied, "Yes, my friend, there is, and I apologize for imposing my mood onto you. There is something weighing very heavily on me and I'm in a quandary as to how I can proceed." He turned down the corners of his mouth, considering whether he should impose further on this good man, but he knew Scrooge relied on Cratchit's good sense, so he decided to forge ahead.

Meanwhile, Cratchit had kept silent, giving Carter a chance to collect his thoughts and to decide whether the clerk could be trusted.

"Mr. Cratchit, have you ever lost what meant most to you in the world, due to your own actions?" Cratchit scratched his chin and slowly shook his head from side to side, pondering the question and finding that he had not. It occurred to him that it was perhaps because his life had been so ordinary — so predictable — that he had never had the chance to gamble on something with stakes of that magnitude. He supposed it was a blessing, but one never knew. It might be that he had missed out on some of life's intensity by being mediocre but, if that were the case, so be it. He could not regret that he had never lost anything, or anyone, who was dear to him simply because his behavior tended to be unimaginative.

"Well, I have," said Mr. Carter, "and I am ruing the day I ever did so, although I can't for the life of me see what I could have done differently without reaping the same result. You see, before I sailed for America I was very much in love with a fine woman, but she remained here. It was inconceivable that she could go with me, a penniless man with no prospects other than his own determination and willingness to work. In addition, she believed having a wife would be an additional burden to me as I attempted to better myself. I am also convinced that, had I remained in England, I would still have lost her, either by her eventual disgust with my constant failures, or worse, had we married, by being forced to live in abject poverty, which would no doubt have been our lot. At any rate, we promised to wait for each other, but we lost touch years ago, and that was that." Neither man looked at the other since this information was so intimate and painful. Mr. Carter eventually continued.

"I suppose I am, to many, the proverbial warrior who has returned triumphant, but my life is empty. All of my success means nothing, because I am alone. I do not want anyone else, but I do not know where to find her." He looked at Cratchit apologetically and ventured, "Mr. Cratchit, can you pull on any of that common sense for which you are so famous, and give me hope? What would you do, in my position?"

Cratchit pressed his lips together before pulling his ear and answering. "You know, Mr. Carter, perhaps the best place to start is where you last saw her."

"I've done that, my good man. I've done that. Her rooms are occupied by a different family and they have never heard of her. There is also a new landlord who was bent on being as rude as possible. In fact, he was so hostile that he said I should be grateful that 'the wench scarpered,' because women were always 'more trouble than they were worth.'" Cratchit noted that Carter had made a fist as he said, "I tell you, Cratchit, I wanted to crack his skull, speaking that way about someone he did not know — someone I love." He shook his head, "But that would not have improved my situation, and time in prison would have lessened, rather than increased, my chances of finding her."

"Then logic would say that you have not searched enough corners of this City," said Cratchit. "She must have had friends, relatives, employers – favorite sites or vendors she visited regularly?"

Mr. Carter's face lit with hope. "Excellent thought! I don't recall her friends, and she had no family here, but she was employed. Yes, by Jupiter, she was employed! I'll try there, my perceptive friend. Immediately. I'll try there!" He grabbed Cratchit's hand and pumped it hard. "Thank you, my man. Thank you!", and with that he leaped out the door and was away with the enthusiasm and energy of a youth in love.

CHAPTER ELEVEN

Flora and Dr. Kaye

Catherine was bearing up with more strength and courage than even she expected, yet she did relent when Scrooge insisted that she enlist Flora to visit her for at least a fortnight, and possibly longer. Catherine's godmother had died when Catherine was still a child, so, following their mother's death, both girls resided with Flora's godmother, a Mrs. Kench, in Bloomsbury.

Catherine eventually married, and Flora continued to reside with Mrs. Kench, which meant the sisters were easily within reach of each other for frequent visits. The girls had been left a certain amount of money and it had proven to be sufficient since it had been controlled until they reached the required age, and both tended to be prudent in their spending.

Although Catherine was the elder by near three years, the two women were like twins. They were connected not only by birth and blood, but by an understanding of each other that could not be explained. Often one would begin a sentence only to have the other give its completion. They always rightly understood each other, no matter how wrongly a sentence may have been phrased, and they displayed a strong family resemblance in their countenance and bearing. There were some differences, however. Where Catherine might hesitate in order to choose an appropriate response, Flora was more likely to be led by her heart, which was prone to outbursts. It was that particular aspect of her character that would, no doubt, respond to the news of Fred.

Catherine requested that Flora come for tea the very afternoon of Uncle Scrooge's tragic announcement, in order to tell her the sad news in person. She would not inform her of such a thing in a cold, flat letter. It would not do. She knew, too, that Flora would simply come to her immediately upon reading the letter, so she might as well tell her to her face, rather than have her running about town in the state of upset that only Flora could generate.

Over tea and biscuits Catherine broke the news to her sister in the calmest and most loving way she could muster, considering her own state of mind. She hoped to soften the blow, but the instant she uttered the word "dead," Flora's hands flew to her mouth. Taking a quick breath, she began to sob. Then she wailed, and eventually stood in order to pace the room. This she managed to do in one continuous motion, leaving Catherine to observe from her chair. She knew Flora was not acting, although anyone who was not acquainted with her may have assumed she was trying for a part on stage. It was one of the things that had always oddly endeared her to Catherine. In fact, during happier times, Flora's antics, sincere as they might be, had often brought Catherine a great deal of levity. Just now, however, she could not laugh, and she was unsure as to how she would ever get through this. She might be required to request that Flora act in more of a calm manner, if that were possible.

As if designed to interrupt her thoughts, Flora suddenly collapsed hysterically at Catherine's feet, threw her head in Catherine's lap and cried, through sobs and hiccups, "Oh . . . Sister . . . (gulp), wha-hat are we (hic) to . . . doooo?" Catherine did not know. She had no plan but knew she would take one step at a time until her child was born, and then she would simply be the best mother she could possibly be. She would live for Fred's child since she could no longer live for him.

"Now, Flora," she admonished, more firmly than she had ever done. Lifting her by the arms, Catherine urged, "Get up from the floor and let's take a sensible approach to this terrible thing we are facing. We must do it together and we must do it with dry eyes, whenever possible, and clear minds." With the solemn expression of a serious elder, she added, "I trust you understand me." Flora nodded, still hiccupping, and dried her eyes. She understood. She must prepare herself to assist Catherine as a grown woman, or she would be no good to her dear sister and her precious offspring. Flora would later look back on this particular exchange as an important moment in her life, for it was when she chose to at least make the attempt to put childish and useless antics aside.

Flora was willing and determined to remain with Catherine, and during their first few days together the women forged a meaningful and amiable schedule. For that reason, it was mutually agreed that Flora's visit should extend indefinitely. Days were spent on occasional walks, but visitors were discouraged by the black wreath that now hung on the front door, and the letters they received were answered, but any invitations were politely declined. Flora had been informed of the coming child and swore solemnly that it would remain their secret for the time being. The sisters sat comfortably together in the evenings, one or both of them sewing or reading, ever planning for the child who would come in the autumn.

Scrooge appeared at the Symons home daily, for at least a short visit, and Catherine was managing as a new widow who hid her grief from everyone, save those closest to her, and even from them most of the time. Her eyes were often red when she emerged from her room after a nap, but she refused to admit she had been in tears. She believed her grief should be mostly expressed alone. It was odd how she often felt nearest to Fred when she mourned the most, as if the pain were some sort of connection to him. She couldn't explain it, so she made no attempt to do so, but it was somehow an excruciating and unlikely means of keeping him close to her. She almost dreaded the time when she might no longer weep for him, because it could mean that he was departing from her memory. She knew it made no sense, but the thought of no longer shedding tears made her shed them all the more.

C3&O

On the days when Dr. Kaye called, he spent little time with Catherine since she was progressing so well. He did confirm that the baby would likely come in late October, which pleased Catherine. It would mean the child's birthday would not be in direct competition with the Baby Jesus' nativity, and she would be sufficiently recovered from her lying-in to manage some sort of Christmas dinner for Uncle Scrooge and Flora. It had long been planned that she and Fred would host this year's Christmas Day dinner, and she was determined to do so, even though she wondered, at times, how on earth she would get through it. Although she was unaware of the process taking place within her soul, Catherine was gradually becoming a very resilient and practical woman.

Catherine knew the physician was confidently at ease regarding her condition, but there was something on her mind and she decided to broach the subject with him. He was, after all, older and very experienced, and had always treated her very kindly. See was certain he would never simply dismiss her concerns as mere "hysteria."

"Doctor," began Catherine. "I have a further question, but I am fearful of speaking it aloud lest I somehow bring it to pass by uttering it." It was clear that Catherine was doing her best not to be upset, but something was disconcerting. "Can you tell me how common is the occurrence of a woman dying in childbirth? I know you will say that I am young and fit, but I see young and fit women succumbing to the birth of a child fairly consistently. Is there something they all seem to have in common?"

The physician's usual response to this very question was exactly as she had just said, and now, thanks to her, he could not say it as if he were imparting new information. So, he simply agreed on both points. "Yes, Catherine, you are correct, but that is because it is the young and fit who are usually giving birth. Still, I am frequently asked this question, even by the husbands." He wanted to bite his tongue since Fred would not be asking anything, but quickly added, "I can only say to you that I do not expect any difficulties, and the majority of births do not have complications." Then he completed his answer by saying, "I am also employing newer methods of hygiene, which I believe may contribute to healthier mothers and babies." That was precisely the sort of statement Catherine was hoping for because it gave her the opportunity to make a statement.

"Dr. Kaye, speaking of newer practices, I am quite determined that I shall not have my blood drawn. I do not believe it is in anyone's best interests to lose one's blood at any time, much less in childbirth, and I will brook no argument on the subject." The physician was taken aback by Catherine's adamant declaration, but he did not argue. If she needed to be bled in order to prevent inflammation, he would simply do what he thought best when the time came, and that was that. No patient had yet dictated to him, and this slip of a girl would not be the first to do so! Since he did not respond to her demand, Catherine took his silence as agreement.

"Thank you, Doctor. I know you cannot see into the future and I know you are telling me the truth, but it isn't so much for my own safety that I have been concerned. It is, you see, not so important that I live, other than that no one wants a child to grow up without both parents, but I desperately want this child of Fred's to live – to grow strong in all aspects and to represent his or her father to the world. Tell me, is there any way of predicting — oh, I know there isn't — whether a mother and her child would both die?" She knew she wasn't asking sensible questions and could not, therefore, expect sensible answers. Poor doctor!

Catherine needn't have been concerned, since Dr. Kaye had been through these sorts of questions for decades. He simply patted her arm, told her not to fret herself, and bid her good day. He knew that was easier said than done, but he had nothing else to offer, and the truth was, he occasionally grew weary of dealing with women's frenzies. Why on earth could they not be more like men?

CHAPTER TWELVE

The Funeral

O nce the secret was out, it took no time for the whole of London to know that Fred Symons, of Scrooge and Symons, was dead. When the death notice was posted in the newspaper, readers considered it old news. Fred was widely known socially and as a businessman, and those who were acquainted with him personally, or even only by reputation, clicked their tongues and said what a terrible loss it was; how he was too good and too young to die, and that they could not understand how or why it happened. Naturally, the cause of his death had been exaggerated tenfold by the rumor mongers, and at the last it was generally accepted that he had been set upon and murdered for his purse while on a ship to the Continent, and that Scrooge had somehow retrieved what was nothing more than a battered and desecrated body, to bury.

The Symons household was in mourning, which naturally included the servants. No one seemed to mind the social restrictions since all had been very fond of the master and were deeply sorry to lose him. However, Catherine, and Fred when he was alive, had been willing to disregard some of society's demands regarding "proper" behavior, and this occasion would be no different. Although she would continue to wear mourning clothes, Catherine would not insist the servants wear black once the funeral had taken place. She also made it very clear that there was to be life and laughter in the home. She believed that joy was a better testament to her husband than spending all day with dour expressions, acting as though there were no such thing as a wonderful afterlife, where she was certain he had gone. She was also set on creating a congenial atmosphere for her new child.

At least there was a black wreath on the door. The new widow had also ordered black-rimmed stationery, which she would use for all of her correspondence, but she forbade the servants to cover mirrors or to keep the blinds drawn. "Fred would not want it that way," she explained. "He knew we all cared for him, and so do all those who are acquainted with us, so it is unnecessary for us to wallow in a display of grief simply to make a show of it. Our grief is real enough and letting the sunlight into a room will remind me of the sunlight in Fred's character." The servants simply nodded at the proclamation, but were decidedly relieved, and pleased that they would not be required to go about in mourning clothes and downcast attitudes in order to prove how much they had cared for their master.

From what Norris was able to glean, Fred did not appear to have died violently, although the surgeon was unwilling to settle on an exact cause of death. He suggested anything from a damaged liver to the usual occurrences such as the grippe, or apoplexy, and he did not think it necessary to order an inquest. Due to the state of the body, and the fact that the surgeon did not immediately release it, planning a funeral had been somewhat complicated, if not downright difficult.

Scrooge had guided Catherine as much as possible, but there were some issues that took a bit of convincing. For one thing, the circumstances dictated that it was not practical to bring the body to the house, even though that was the general practice. Catherine had expected to view the remains of her beloved one last time and was dismayed at the prospect of never looking upon him again. Scrooge, on the other hand, desperately wanted to keep her from seeing the corpse in its current condition.

Following several conversations, Scrooge finally put an end to it by imploring Catherine with, "My dear, it simply will not do. As your guardian of sorts, I cannot allow you to see Fred in this state. It will not edify, and I must insist that you recall him as he was in life." She recognized that this was his final word on the subject and, because she trusted him, she acceded to his wishes. There would be no funeral in the home and she would never again see Fred's face, or lay her hand on his. All of this she managed to bear by imagining the eventuality of holding his child in her arms.

In order to avoid improper incidents such as those he had heard tell of regarding the practices of undertakers, Scrooge engaged men who were recommended to him as the most reliable in London. They would prepare the body for burial and transport it directly to the Church of St. Michael, where the funeral would be held. It was also well-known that the men hired to transport the coffin, as well as the grave diggers, could be heavy imbibers who often engaged in all sorts of misbehavior, even causing injury. For that reason, Scrooge spurned the idea of a night funeral, saying it was far too dangerous. Catherine suggested that the service be held in late morning, with a luncheon following at the Symons home, by invitation.

It was agreed that black horses would pull the hearse. Scrooge also wished to observe the custom of following the hearse on foot from the church to the private cemetery, and several men had asked to join him. He had convinced Catherine not to attend, and certainly not to follow the hearse on foot, not only because it could be thought by some to be improper for a lady to do so, but most importantly because she was with child. It did not take much to garner her agreement since the child was the highest priority for both of them. Catherine would not be alone, however, because the women would be invited to join her at her home while the men were at the funeral.

Scrooge refused to hire mourners, preferring instead to have genuine mourners and pallbearers at the proceedings – people who had truly cared for Fred. Among those would be himself, Cratchit, Homer, Julian Thorne, Dick Wilkins, and Constable Norris, if he were available. Edwin Carter had also requested to be included, even though he had only known Fred since Carter's return from America. Scrooge knew there would be many more attending the services since Fred had many friends who would want to honor him.

Even though they came on a good recommendation, to assuage his misgivings concerning the undertakers, Scrooge insisted on viewing the body prior to the funeral. It was not a pleasant thing to once again gaze on his nephew in death, but all seemed to be in order. Fred's face had been shaved, his hair combed, and his body had not been robbed of its suit!

There was only one mishap, and it occurred at the cemetery after the casket had been lowered into the grave. Since it was a private cemetery Scrooge was hoping there would be no misbehavior by the gravediggers. Unfortunately, in keeping with all of the sordid tales Scrooge had heard concerning their habits, one of them had imbibed enough gin that morning to make him foolhardy most of the day. Unaware that he was acting prematurely, as soon as the Rector recited, "Earth to earth, ashes to ashes, dust to dust," he quickly approached the grave through a gap between the mourners and tossed a shovel-full of dirt onto the casket. Wilkins yelled, "Here, man, what do you think you're doing?", which alerted the digger's companion to the fact that there was a problem. The second digger was somewhat less inebriated but had, himself, swallowed enough gin to render his equilibrium questionable. Nevertheless, to make a show of setting things to rights, he laid hold of the shovel handle and attempted to wrest it away from his partner.

"Ere," he admonished. "You can't be doin' that now. The rekter's still rattlin' on!" His remark was met with an, "Ow! Don' be pushin'," and before anyone could successfully latch on to either of them, they toppled into the grave, landing resoundingly in a drunken heap on the coffin, all the while swearing loudly at each other for their clumsiness.

Wilkins and Carter reached down to pull them out, but they were "dead" weights and unable to effectively assist in climbing out of the grave. As in a game of tug-of-war, more men assisted by forming two chains – one behind Wilkins, and one behind Carter. They hauled the gravediggers out, dragged them as far away from the proceedings as possible, and left them to their derision of each other.

Rector Gifford continued as if there had been no interruption, and at the appropriate moment several mourners tossed their handfuls of earth onto the already dirty casket, all the while ignoring the gravediggers' distant exchange of insults. Scrooge was thoroughly disgusted with them both and vowed to later verify that they had, in fact, completed the task of burying Fred. He wished he had the means to deal with their abominable behavior, but he knew that would be near impossible. Thank goodness Catherine had remained at home!

୧୫୬୦

Although appropriately solemn, the funeral luncheon was a congenial and elegant affair, befitting the man, himself. Catherine greeted each guest, ensuring that they were comfortable and well-fed. As each one took her hand and uttered statements that were meant to be consoling, she managed to keep most of her tears at bay, but occasionally she felt the need to scream. None of this could bring back her husband, and often she could think of nothing new to say in reply.

So, mostly she resorted to a simple, "Thank you, that means so much." Still, in the midst of her own discomfort, Catherine was thankful for how well-liked and respected Fred had been.

Following the luncheon, Catherine stood visiting with Marian Thorne, whose husband Julian had been such a dear friend to Fred, when Mrs. Langstone approached. Smiling at both women and begging their pardon, she placed her hand lightly on Catherine's forearm and said, "When you are available, I wonder if I may speak with you privately." Mrs. Thorne saw no reason why they shouldn't speak right then, so she made the excuse that she needed to see to her husband's whereabouts, and kindly left them alone. Mrs. Langstone's request actually pleased Catherine since she had intended to have a conversation with her at the earliest opportunity, but she did not expect to have it that day. She guided Mrs. Langstone with an outstretched arm and they slipped into Fred's library, where they both sat in comfortable overstuffed chairs. Mrs. Langstone began.

"I do hope you will forgive me, Catherine (if I may use your given name), because I do not want to overstep, but I must ask you a question. I ask not only out of curiosity, but because I pray I can be of assistance."

Catherine could not imagine what possible question Mrs. Langstone could ask, but she agreed, of course, because she trusted her and knew she was asking out of true concern. "Yes, and please, do call me Catherine." She would not, however, ask the same of Mrs. Langstone, because she was Catherine's elder and a particular friend of Uncle Scrooge's.

There was no sense in prolonging the moment, so Mrs. Langstone came out with it. "I do again beg your pardon but . . . are you with child?"

Catherine was shocked, but not offended. *How could she have known?* "Oh, I think I understand. You have been speaking with Uncle Scrooge, is that correct?" Realizing she had not answered the question, Catherine quickly added, "Yes, I am to have a child this autumn, but I have neither husband nor mother, to help me," and with that, she burst into tears. It was amazing how many tears the body could produce, but she was certain she had shed a barrel-full since learning Fred's fate.

"No, my dear. I have not spoken with your uncle on this subject, so, if he was sworn to secrecy, you may rest assured that he kept faith. I simply took note of your appearance and read what I believed to be the signs of impending motherhood. Even in your grief I saw a beauty about you that I have seen in many women who are carrying a new life. I believe it was even so, in my case." Displaying a very sincere and sympathetic smile, Mrs. Langstone entreated, "I do hope you will allow me to offer assistance during this time, and even through your lying-in. I believe I can furnish information and, I pray, some comfort. I cannot replace your mother, my dear, but I can be a friend." Catherine was smiling bravely through tears that still clouded her eyes.

For a reason she could not have explained, Mrs. Langstone felt it might be helpful if she related some of her own history to Catherine.

"You see, I am not entirely unacquainted with the loss of loved ones, and I have been a mother, so I am also aware of that miraculous process." Not wanting to give Catherine too much information on

114

which to ruminate, Mrs. Langstone simply said, "I lost my son when he was six years of age, and my husband four years following." Responding to Catherine's expression of heartfelt sympathy, she smiled and said, "I am recovered enough to carry on and even enjoy my life, but I can never return to the person I once was. One doesn't, you know, so I completely understand the tears and your belief that life is over. I am also certain that, since you are carrying your husband's child, that gives you great reason to plan for the future."

Catherine was so relieved to have someone who understood the actualities of birth, and loss, that she clutched both of Mrs. Langstone's hands in hers. While making a great effort not to cry again, she whispered a very grateful, "Thank you. Thank you so much. I'm very appreciative, and I look forward to having you by my side in welcoming Fred's child to the family."

It was exactly what Catherine had hoped, and from this very person. Having staunched her earlier tears, she now broke out in grateful sobs, which caused Mrs. Langstone to weep with her.

CHAPTER THIRTEEN

Rector Colin Gifford

The Sunday following the funeral found Scrooge in his usual pew in the Church of St. Michael. It was the very nave where Fred's service had been conducted by Rector Gifford, who was now preparing to deliver his weekly homily.

Scrooge was beyond unhappy. He was devastated, but he had learned during the first year of his redemption that it would be foolhardy to return to his previous state of selfishness and bitterness. He prayed that the future would, with time, bring an ease to this pain. So, he stood with the rest and sang songs of praise and hope, but he felt nothing but emptiness. The only spark of true hope he could muster came from thoughts of Catherine and Fred's baby. She stood beside him now, bravely singing along, and their presence gave each other a certain comfort, which did not at all bring healing. Finally, they sat, and

Scrooge prepared himself to make every attempt to stay awake during the sermon.

The Rector stood in the pulpit and began. "My dear friends, we live in perilous times." He paused before adding, "I realize you are thinking, 'How can that be, Rector? We are not facing invasion, our monarchy is settled, and there is no famine in the land,' and those things are all certainly true. It is also true that any clergyman at any time throughout history, and at any time in the future, could make the same statement, and it would apply. Humanity always exists in perilous times because of the war between good and evil that swarms around, and within, each of us. We face good and evil, and we choose which way to go. The thing we must keep in mind is that our choices are generally governed either by faith, or fear."

Scrooge was jerked to attention. *There it is again! First Marley, then Priscilla, and now the Rector has said that faith is a choice that can make a difference. Was it my imagination, or was the Rector looking directly at me most of the time he was speaking?*

Although he did not fall asleep, Scrooge heard little of the remainder of the sermon, but what little he had heard was burned into his brain. *Fear, or faith. But of what am I afraid? The thing I feared most has already occurred, so what is left to frighten me? Am I afraid of being alone? Could that be what is driving me to Mrs. Langstone, rather than a true attachment?* He needed to examine what, exactly, could be fearful, and what on God's green earth he could do about it. Perhaps the Rector could help. He would attempt to see him that very afternoon!

CஃBᘓᏅ

Scrooge liked Rector Gifford very much and enjoyed his company immensely. They had spent many hours together, engaged in meaningful and rewarding conversations, and even played the occasional game of chess. They seemed to win equally, which proved to Scrooge that they were evenly matched, not only in temperament and interests, but in strategic skills. So, it was natural for Scrooge to turn to his friend for spiritual assistance. He trusted the man, and always heard good sense from him.

"Now, my friend," said the Rector. "This does not seem to be purely a social call, so I must presume there is something on your mind. You know I am always willing to broach most any subject, particularly from you, since it is often intriguing."

Scrooge appreciated the man's no-nonsense approach to the matters of life. It made it much easier to bare one's soul and get to the heart of what was truly going amiss.

"Rector," began Scrooge, "I am a man without much hope. You have seen me in this state before, but this time I believe I have nothing left to lose, and that puts me as good as in the grave." He knew he sounded dramatic, but he felt it, so why not make it plain to the Rector as quickly as possible. It wouldn't, after all, be quite fair to make the Rector work to get to the truth of the matter, so Scrooge decided to tell him straight off, in as logical a manner as he could manage.

"As you well know, my nephew and heir has died, and is buried. You are also aware that we do not know how, or even where it occurred, other than that it was most likely in the North. Then, his body was placed on a barge and sent here, to London. It appears he did not die in the Netherlands, where he was to be at the time, and his death, apart from being an appalling catastrophe, is a total mystery. I am not only heartbroken, I am perplexed. Other than the fact that his widow is expecting their child, I am left with absolutely no expectations. I have been plunged from a happiness I thought I would never know, to a depth of despair such as I would not wish on anyone." The rector was a patient man and didn't like to interrupt, so he nodded and let Scrooge continue.

"There is, however, a theme that has presented itself on three occasions now, and I am hoping you can explain it, at least in part." He would not admit that his dead partner's ghost was the first one to utter the words, so he simply said, "You are the third person to say to me, in essence, that I must choose between fear and faith in my dealings with people and, I suppose, with life in general. I understand the concepts, but I am unable to control, much less apply them."

Here Scrooge decided to tell a bit more. "Rector, there is another ingredient in the mix that I should relate. I am very much enamored with a unique and delightful woman. I suspect that she cares for me, but I haven't the courage, or perhaps the commitment to the possibilities, as well as confidence in my own feelings, to do anything about it. Perhaps I am too old to form an intimate bond. Would our love last for the rest of our lives? I may even be imagining we could eventually marry only because I am, with the loss of Fred, fearful of being alone - and so on." Finally, he admitted, "Having lost my nephew, I am at sea on all subjects, and that includes my feelings for this very special woman. I do not know how to proceed with the business of living!"

The Rector smiled. He was very fond of Scrooge and knew his heart to be devoted to doing good and being kind. He also knew Scrooge could be bull-headed, even a bit rash, but he was always sincere. The Rector began by saying, "You are currently grieving, and that, in itself, colors everything about your life. It is natural that you would find it difficult to proceed with anything, given that sorrow. However, I don't believe that grief, itself, is based in fear, other than the uncertainty of how to carry on without that certain person. Grief can paralyze for a season, but, at some point faith must arise and once again carry you forward. It is also possible to be afraid and yet proceed in faith. When fear 'replaces' faith, however, it can prevent you from acting, and it can also force you to act in ways you should not.

"The one thing you do not want to do is act foolishly out of fear and, to that end, I want to tell you a story." Both men settled back as the Rector began what Scrooge knew would be one of his lengthy, yet engaging tales.

"When I was a young man I was courting a girl who I thought was the loveliest, most charming person in the world. I was totally besotted, and she knew it. I believe she knew it before I did, because she seemed able to predict the things I would do for her, and the things I wanted to say to her, but never could." He took a bite of biscuit and offered the plate to Scrooge while he chewed. The Rector swallowed, took a drink of tea, and continued.

"We were riding in one of my father's carts one day and she talked me into taking a route we had never used before, so I was apprehensive about getting lost or somehow having a mishap. There were several things in my mind, all of which came under the title 'Fear.' I did not want to appear inadequate in her eyes; I did not want to damage my father's cart; I did not want to get lost, nor did I want to have to admit any of those thoughts to her.

"I was driving the horse up a slight incline in a wooded area and could not see 'round the next bend, but fear told me there was a dangerous drop-off waiting. Rather than discounting the possibility, or simply having faith that we could easily navigate it at a slow speed, I let my mind imagine all of the horrid possibilities that were lying in wait, just ahead. As my fear grew, I envisioned losing control; having a serious upset; killing the horse, or one of us; my father disowning me; being an outcast and my life ending – either by dying outright, or by being rejected by society." They both smiled at the youthful silliness, although both realized that fear had a way of affecting even the most mature in the same manner.

"By the time we approached the curve I was so flustered and disturbed that I could not speak, and was gripping the reins for all I was worth! The horse sensed my misgivings and began to resist my directives, picking up speed. It's interesting that fear, when combined with pride, can bring disaster. I had become so bent on proving I was unafraid that I allowed the beast into a near run, gritting my teeth for what was to come. The lady sensed my fear and she, herself, became fearful of my recklessness. Every time she begged me to slow the cart

I dithered between giving the animal more rein and attempting to exert some control. By the time we rounded the corner we were both petrified and the cart barely remained on the path. There was no cliff, but we very nearly careened off the track, which could have been disastrous, at any rate.

"She was furious, and I was furious with myself. We refused to speak to each other the rest of the way home, even though I had, by then, slowed the horse to a nice walk. Naturally she refused to ride with me again, and our romance that was just beginning to bud died before the bloom. I have never forgotten my foolishness, which was totally driven by fear — fear of a cliff that did not exist, and fear of showing my fear - which made me reckless." He shifted in his chair, preparing to continue.

"The question exists, would she and I eventually have married, had I not been so imprudent as to let fear, fueled by pride, take over the situation? One can't know, but I do know that it was my actions that ended the friendship, rather than a natural drifting apart. When she saw how I was behaving she became gripped with fear too, and it didn't end when we rounded the bend in the path. She no longer trusted me to always act in a rational manner. I had endangered her life and she did not believe I would always protect her. In her eyes I was a fool."

The Rector cleared his throat. "I often wondered how fear could encourage me to do the very thing that might bring about what I dreaded, but then, being fearful can somehow manage to make us work against ourselves and our best interests, can it not?" Scrooge nodded.

He knew it was true but was not yet certain how to apply all of this to his own situation.

As if wrapping up a sermon, the Rector said, "I will end with this. Since the death of your nephew you may have concluded that you have nothing left in your life in which to invest faith, and that, in itself, could be cause for fear, but you do have cause for faith. I will state the obvious – Fred is gone, but you are here, and you remain for a reason. You are still the patriarch of the family and you will continue to guide Catherine, and even others, such as the Cratchits. Soon you will be assisting in the rearing of Fred's child. All of that will require a great deal of faith, and I believe that it will, also, in the doing, bring joy."

Scrooge must ask, "This is all well and good, but how do I know whether I am acting out of fear, or faith?"

"Ah, my good man," smiled the Rector. "That is an excellent question, and I believe I have an excellent answer for you. There is a simple test. When you are feeling the urge to act on something, ask yourself one question. 'Do I feel a Godly peace about this, or do I feel unrest and angst?' If it is the latter, you are very likely being driven by fear. I should add that, if you are not definitively inclined to either peace or disquietude, simply do not act until you have a true calm about your decision. A bit of advice I always give is, 'When in doubt - don't.'" Looking at Scrooge he asked, "Perhaps you can even apply a few of these simple principles in your relationship with your dear lady?"

Scrooge gave a half smile that revealed nothing, but the Rector understood.

CHAPTER FOURTEEN

An Intruder

S everal days following the funeral, Catherine and Flora ate a light supper and spent the remainder of the evening in the parlor. Flora played the piano and Catherine allowed Teague to sit on her lap while she still had the semblance of one. It had been a pleasant evening, and now that the funeral and burial were concluded, things would no doubt settle. Catherine was not convinced she could ever return to "normal" without Fred, knowing her life would never be the same. Were it not for the coming child, she did not know how she would go on.

The servants had been released early as a reward for dealing so well with the houschold bustle between Fred's death and his funeral. They had performed without complaint and done an excellent job, and Catherine wanted them to know how much she appreciated them.

Since her maid was dismissed for the evening, the sisters had assisted each other in disrobing and preparing for bed. Against general etiquette they then sat downstairs, very cozily, in their dressing gowns. Flora had just finished a somewhat melancholic piece at the piano and announced she was going to retire. It seemed a good idea.

Flora suggested, "Catherine, I can easily put down the lights if you will proceed to your bed. I expect you are weary and could use some good sleep. Would you like a cup of warm milk?"

Catherine shook her head and said, "Thank you, Flora, but I believe I will have need of nothing to help me sleep tonight. I admit I have not slept well for many days, but now that everything is done, I suspect my rest will come easier." Calling her Spaniel to her, she added, "Teague will keep me company, and we shall sleep the sleep of the dead." Realizing what she had just said, Catherine allowed the tears to well in her eyes, but none fell. She was doing better now and was less prone to quite so many fits of grief. Flora's heart ached for her, but all she could do was be as good a companion as she was able, and attempt to keep Catherine's mind on other things.

No sound came from the servants' quarters. Assuming everyone was asleep, Catherine entered her own chamber and climbed into bed. Were she to be perfectly honest, she would admit that one reason sleep had been eluding her was because she was frightened. She had never been quite so afraid while Fred was alive, even when he was away, but since the finality of his death the nights had been extremely long and lonely, even eerie. In the depths of the night everything seemed immensely cold, dark, and menacing, with all of the house's groans, creaks, and shadows that appeared to dart from here to there. Once she had even gone to the window to ensure that a set of inky spots on her wall was actually a silhouette from a tree. Other shapes were not so easily explained. She refused to believe that Fred's ghost was wandering about, and he certainly would not haunt her, but there were those odd contours that seemed to have no origin . . .

Most nights Catherine left one light lit in her room, not only for herself, but also for Teague, who seemed to be somewhat excitable these days. Tonight, however, she chose to be courageous and she turned out all of her lamps. The house was very still, and Catherine could certainly manage. She must get used to sleeping in the same manner as any other normal person. She must, and she would! It was dark and strangely quiet, but she reminded herself that she was safely locked in her home.

All went well for an hour or so, even though Catherine could not keep her eyes closed for more than a few moments. Then she heard a new, and different, noise.

Was that a rattle? Surely not. It was definitely a sound from the servants' quarters, above. I mustn't keep imagining things! Fred would laugh at me and say I was being silly, but it's as if my ears have increased their abilities a hundred-fold. I suspect I'm now hearing things that are happening outside and half a mile away.

Soon she heard the rattle again and would have sworn it was the opening of a door downstairs. Did Flora hear it, too? If not, it was certainly Catherine's own imagination. This must stop! If she went on like this until her delivery she would be unfit to welcome a child into the world, much less care for it, but she seemed unable to stifle her imaginings. She turned onto her side, muffling one ear with the pillow, and pulled her covers over the other ear, but it did no good. Suddenly she was sitting up, listening again.

Footsteps! Were those footsteps? Yes! That was the creaky stair that just squeaked, I'm certain of it. Someone — or something — is coming . . . up . . . the . . . stairs!!!

Catherine unwittingly opened her mouth to scream, but nothing came out, just like in a bad dream. Where was Flora? Was she safe? Had she managed to turn down the lights and get to her bedchamber safely? How could Catherine find out? Perhaps, if she peeked out the door, she could dart to Flora's room and reassure herself that all was well. Yes, that was what she would do. Wrapping her night cloak about her, she tip-toed to the door, followed by Teague, and slowly opened it. No one was about. Without giving it another thought, she darted silently across the hallway to Flora's room, ran in and shut the door behind her. She did not realize Teague had remained in the hallway.

"What is it? What's wrong?", cried Flora, as she sat up in bed. There were no lamps lit in her room, but there was just enough ambient light to allow them to see each other's outlines. "I'll light the lamp," said Flora, but Catherine gave an urgent, "Shhhhhhhh," and loudly whispered "NO! Don't light anything! I believe we have an intruder downstairs."

Now Flora was afraid, and neither of them knew what to do. Should they cry for the servants, or would that alert the intruder to their whereabouts? If his intent was to harm them he would know their exact location from their screams and could easily reach them before the servants could save them.

Just then Teague began to yap or, as Fred used to say, "bark his fool head off." The yapping was loud and frantic, and they could tell by the sound that he was running in circles in the hallway. What was happening? Was he being chased? Hurt? Worse?? His barking then echoed down the stairs and stopped abruptly. *Oh, no! They've killed him! Oh, my poor, sweet pup. He's been butchered, trying to protect us! Poor, poor Teague.*

Without explaining herself, Catherine clutched Flora's hand, yanked her up and the two of them flew silently back to her own room. It seemed the safest place, for some reason. On her way out, Flora grabbed her umbrella, wishing it were a cricket bat.

The women huddled together in Catherine's room, praying that the intruder, or intruders, would find enough valuables downstairs that they would be satisfied, and leave, but soon the footsteps resumed. Whoever it was must have gone back down, looked around and killed Teague to silence him, and were now coming back up to kill them, too! Flora was visibly shaking, and it was all Catherine could do to prevent her from crying out. When the doorknob began to rotate, and the bedroom door slowly opened, Catherine finally found her own voice. She let out a scream loud enough to wake the entire household, and was joined by Flora, whose ear-splitting shriek may have been heard as far as Hampstead Heath. It did not deter the intruder, however.

Unable to move, they found themselves staring at a horrifying apparition! It was the ghastly mask of a corpse – terrifying in its appearance - and it momentarily paralyzed both Catherine and Flora. As it moved into the room the women managed to jump up to run, but since the way out was blocked by the apparition, they bumped into each other instead, and continued pushing and screaming as they ran to and fro, searching for an escape. Flora finally gathered her wits enough to grab the umbrella, and began to thrash the thing, hoping to chase it away. Amid all of the commotion, Teague reappeared, barking very loudly and consistently, adding greatly to the tumult.

Naturally the servants came running, having been awakened by the screams and the ensuing clamor. They discovered the scene of the uproar and created their own disturbance with cries of confusion. By then the apparition had also begun to shout. "Catherine! Catherine!! Flora, stop bashing me! What in the name of . . . Stop, I say! Stop!! Would you all please cease this commotion - immediately!"

It took a moment to realize that it was not an apparition, but was actually the master of the house — Fred Symons — in the flesh! Having been unwilling to take the effort to light lamps, he had chosen a candle instead, and had been holding it at an angle that lit his face from under his chin, giving him the appearance of a sinister and supernatural specter. Flora stopped still, her umbrella poised for another strike, and the shouting died down. The entire company stood motionless, agape at the man until Flora, in what may have been the final hysterical act of her life, doubled over in a dead faint. Catherine fell to her knees, laughing and crying all at once, thanking God, and Fred said simply, "Will someone please explain to me the reason for all of this tumult? And why is there a black wreath on the door?"

The wreath was immediately removed, and it was very late by the time Fred heard the entire tale. Once all had recovered from their discomposure and were able to put a few cogent sentences together, Fred learned that he had been dead, buried and was currently being mourned. Although everyone was overjoyed to see him, his return to life did raise a number of new questions, but those could wait.

Fred wanted to see his Uncle Scrooge and was only prevented by Catherine's reminder that it was the middle of the night. He did not wish to wait until morning, knowing his uncle was suffering with grief, but finally agreed that the poor man was asleep and should be allowed to remain so until morning. Moreover, he and Catherine needed a few hours together, she more than he, if only to stare at him and put her hand in his. Holding his hand was a small, yet meaningful act she had believed she would never do again.

CʒꙄꙊ

Scrooge was not asleep. He had not slept a full night since the beginning of this horrific event. After tossing for several hours, he finally rose to Mrs. Dilber's bustling about, and listened politely while she tried to force him to eat his breakfast.

"Now, Mr. Scrooge, I'm willin' to wager you 'aven't slept well for ages, an' you 'aven't ate enough to keep a hummingbird alive. Look 'ere, Mrs. Haiter made you some nice rolls, an' there's a bit o' bacon to go with 'em. You try 'n eat, Sir. It'll 'elp make things a bit more bearable." Refusing to give up easily, she insisted, "I 'ave some coffee, too, just the way you like it. Now you get some of that down before you go to your office, so's you can do a proper day's work."

Scrooge appreciated her efforts and thanked her, but the only thing that would make him feel better would be to see his nephew walk through the door, sit down, and share the meal. He had only just formed that thought when they both heard the door knocker and Mrs. Dilber moved to answer. Almost immediately she let out such a terrible squeal that Scrooge jumped from his chair and hastened to her rescue. At the entry he found Mrs. Dilber leaning against the open door with her apron over her head, where she had flung it in fright, and standing in the doorway was one who very much resembled his beloved nephew. With a half-smile Fred said, simply, "I understand from my unruly household, and from Mrs. Dilber's terrified reaction, that I am meant to be in the grave."

It took Scrooge a moment. The sight of his nephew standing there, alive and well, breathing London's questionable air, demanded a change of mind. It was an exercise requiring several seconds, but Scrooge recovered quickly because he very much wanted to believe his eyes, and he did not care at that moment how, or why, it could be so.

Fred began to laugh merrily as Scrooge cried, "My boy! Oh, my dear boy! Praise be! Is it really you — alive? Yes! You're not gone from us, after all!" It was generally not done between men, but without giving it any thought he reached out, pulled Fred to him and embraced him tightly for several moments, refusing to let go for fear of losing him again. Like Catherine, he laughed; he cried; and he thanked God, for he who was lost had been found.

The two men shared a hearty breakfast, the serving of which pleased Mrs. Dilber very much. Scrooge related details of the previous weeks, and Fred eventually brought him up to date regarding his trip. The ideas Fred had presented to their contacts were well-received and it appeared that Mr. Carter had, in fact, suggested a viable venture. After their breakfast had been consumed, both men relaxed and tried to formulate some sort of plan to solve the mystery that now faced them.

"First, we must appear at the counting-house," declared Scrooge, "and let the men know that you are, thankfully, very much alive. Naturally, I will also alert Norris to that fact." Using his napkin to wipe a few new tears of relief and joy, Scrooge added, "This definitely puts another angle on the situation, and raises a number of questions, not the least of which is, who on earth did we bury?"

CHAPTER FIFTEEN

A Plan Is Devised

Without sending a prior warning, Scrooge and Fred walked into the counting-house soon after they knew Cratchit and Homer would be hard at work at their stations. As expected, both men were speechless at the sight of Fred, particularly Homer, since he had seen his corpse. Within seconds however, they recovered and quickly jumped from their stools, grabbed his hand in turn to shake it, and exclaimed over and again, "Mr. Symons! Mr. Symons, Sir! Oh, my. Oh, I say. This is a marvel, is it not?" Cratchit finally tamed his tongue enough to declare, "Well, and you are very much alive! Such a welcome sight!" He then wiped his eyes with his handkerchief, blew his nose, and asked, "But, how can this be?"

Scrooge said all would be explained, or at least all that they knew, and he instructed Homer to send notes immediately to Constable Norris and Dick Wilkins, saying:

I am overcome with joy as I inform you that my nephew, Fred, is very much alive! We must confer as to how to proceed, for proceed we must. Please join me and my men at the counting-house at 2:00 o'clock this afternoon. We need to devise a plan, for we have buried an unknown unfortunate.

Scrooge also instructed Homer to refrain from sending more dispatches to the countries Fred had visited, since Fred did not disappear while on his trip. Homer had sent three, but had not yet received replies. Scrooge gladly stated, "Then we won't worry about them since they will simply confirm what we already know, which is that Fred did meet with them at the appointed times and did not fall victim to an untimely end!"

At 2:00 o'clock the men gathered at the offices of Scrooge and Symons. Constable Norris was the first to arrive, with Dick Wilkins close behind, and by the time they were all assembled there had been much hurrahing and back-slapping. They could not contain their laughter and cries of joy as they all met once more, and were no longer missing a man.

Dick Wilkins always knew what was occurring in Town, so it was he who related the hearsay regarding Fred's return from the dead. As Wilkins explained it, "The news has already spread faster than the Great London Fire, and Fred's bolt from the grave is much more a curiosity to the gossips than the news of his death. Each version of his return seems to depend upon the rumor-monger's beliefs concerning the hereafter, so the imagined reasons for, and the means of, his revived state vary." Here Wilkins could not resist a chuckle, and said, "The final version that came to my ears was that Fred had been buried alive, but grave robbers dug him up before he expired altogether. He was then somehow given into the care of a rogue student of the medical arts, who used uncanny means to regenerate his body and his mind." It was worth a laugh and they all knew they would hear many more versions before the escapade died down, to be replaced eventually by new tittle-tattle regarding someone else's misfortunes.

After the group had settled, Scrooge cleared his throat and began the discussion. "Men, hanging over all of our joy is a dark cloud of truth. A man has died, and we don't know who he is. We can only assume, based on how we felt about losing Fred, that his family and friends are experiencing the same grief, but it must be worse for them in that it is very probable that they do not know where he is, and they very likely do not know what's happened to him. We are going to attempt to change all of that."

"But how?" It was Homer. "And where do we begin?"

"Ah," said Scrooge. "Cratchit, my level-headed friend, what do you suggest?"

Cratchit responded. "I have been giving this a great deal of thought, and I believe we should make a list of what we know to be the pieces of this problem. Perhaps something of import, or a pattern, will jump out at us and give a clue as to how we should proceed."

They all agreed that was a good plan, and Homer volunteered to take notes.

Norris began. The facts are, firstly, that we found a body in the barge. Secondly, the man did not appear to have died violently, although the surgeon has been unable to settle on an exact cause of death. He submits that it may have been anything from a damaged liver to the usual occurrences, such as the grippe, or apoplexy. Thirdly, the body was placed into the barge surreptitiously, which suggests something was either not within the law, or someone simply wanted to be rid of it without having to answer questions or pay for burial."

To clarify, Wilkins asked, "Are we saying, then, that this is definitely not a murder?"

"It appears it was not," replied Norris, "unless he was smothered, or choked, because that would be difficult to discern at this point in time, considering the state of his flesh. Murder would be difficult to prove unless we had an eye witness to the fact."

"What else do we know?", asked Scrooge.

"Well," added Norris, "we also know that no one has come forward to report a missing man, or a body that seems to fit our man. The boaters have been no real help, other than to 'admit,' in a manner of speaking, that one of them was paid to turn the other way when someone laid the body in the barge."

As if that triggered a memory, Scrooge exclaimed, "But we do know where that occurred, which narrows our search from all of the North of England to the county of Buckinghamshire!"

Homer was writing as quickly as possible and had resorted to employing a sort of shorthand he had developed for his own use. He only hoped he would be able to decipher it later, should he need to do so.

Fred frowned as a new thought occurred to him. Addressing Norris, he asked, "Did the surgeon say how long he believed the man to have been dead?" He wasn't sure how that bit could assist them in their efforts, but it seemed worth noting.

"The surgeon could not be certain, but he suspected it was at least a week at the time we found him," replied Norris.

Cratchit added, "You also said he was unshaven and wearing worn clothing, which suggests he was of a lower class, or down on his luck at the time of his death." Then he asked, "I think we could assume he may have pawned anything that was worth a few coins, but was he wearing any jewelry, or carrying any sort of love token?" Norris simply shook his head before adding, "No. If he had anything of value I'm sure he was relieved of it by the time he was placed in the boat. If not, Wigley would have pocketed it, no doubt."

"Something else has been niggling at me," said Scrooge, "and that is, why was he placed in that particular barge? Was it happenstance, or was it purposeful? There would really be no way for someone not directly connected with this office to know who had purchased the load, and who had brokered it, nor to whom it would be delivered, unless someone connected to the shipments saw the opportunity to use one particular load to an evil purpose." They all agreed it was worth noting, but very unlikely.

It was Fred who finally stated the obvious. "There is one thing we cannot explain, and although it may be unlikely to provide any answers, I believe it may give us some direction." Every man looked his way as he said, with a note of astonishment, "The man resembled me."

It was true. Scrooge, Homer, and Norris had each believed the man to be Fred Symons and based on Scrooge and Homer's definite recognition of the body, all three would have sworn to it under oath, had there been an inquest. There was no explanation for Fred's look-alike, but perhaps they could use that fact to discover the identity of the dead man. Several ideas were thrown into the mix, even the suggestion that a notice in the newspaper might work, until Wilkins said, "We wouldn't know which paper to use, or whether these people can even read, and what would we say? 'Is anyone missing a dead body that looks like a man who lives in London?'" Everyone laughed, thoroughly enjoying being able to easily do so once again.

Finally, Cratchit made a suggestion. "Gentlemen, on the face of it, what I am about to suggest may seem foolish, but if the boater was telling the truth, we know the geographical area where the body was placed in the barge. Would it be reasonable to assume he died within a mile or two of that vicinity? If he did, people thereabouts must have known him." The men nodded, agreeing with his reasoning.

He continued his line of thought. "I realize I may be stretching things a bit, but suppose Mr. Symons were to walk the streets of nearby settlements on the chance that there might be a reaction to his presence. Particularly if they knew he had died, wouldn't they make some sort of overture upon seeing him? They might tell us his name and point us to his family. We could very likely learn more about his death."

The men agreed this had the makings of a viable plan, particularly since they had come up with no other alternative. Homer quickly produced a map and the group gathered around.

Indicating a spot on the map with his index finger, Norris said, "The boater 'pretends' the body was placed in the barge near the Marsworth Locks – here. It is a little over six miles from Aylesbury, where they took on their cargo. If we make a circle of a mile or so around the locks, we include these villages. It seems likely that someone in that vicinity would have been acquainted with our dead man. We can only hope he or she would be willing to approach and enquire as to what on earth he is doing up and walking around, or where he has been hiding, and we can then request facts regarding his identity, and possibly his death."

It was eventually agreed that Scrooge and Fred would leave Norris to his London duties, and the two of them would take the railroad to Tring, from where they would launch their search in the villages, for "recognition."

He hated to make such a suggestion, but Homer asked, "If Mr. Symons is to be recognized, should he not dress less as a successful businessman, and more as a laborer? I clearly recall what the corpse was wearing, and it was nothing like what Mr. Symons has on his back."

"That is a valid point," replied Scrooge, and Fred interjected, "I believe my tailor might find some clothing that would do. I hope you will all forgive me if I prefer to be outfitted by him, rather than borrow togs from the rag and bone man. I don't mind appearing to be impoverished, but I would prefer not to have fleas." This brought a laugh from the men, and they agreed there might be a middle ground between how Fred was dressed at that moment, and how the man in the barge had been dressed.

Homer apologized as he recalled one other thing. "We mustn't forget that he was also unshaven. Our man didn't wear a full beard, but my guess is that his face hadn't felt a razor for at least a week before his death." Fred's countenance was getting more clouded with each suggestion regarding his appearance, but he knew these were necessary details to what was soon to become a disguise. He could only pray none of his business associates spotted him on the way to the train, or anywhere along the trip.

❦

Fred and Scrooge stood before Fred's tailor, Mr. Meller, resembling schoolboys who had been found out for pulling a wicked prank. The man was aghast at what was being suggested. "Outrage! You ask me to dress you like a mudlark?" In disbelief, he asked, "You want to look like one of those boys who crawl about the Thames, digging up small bits to sell? No! You are a well-turned-out man. I make you look prosperous, like the businessman you are, and I should now make you look like a beggar?" He threw up both hands and exclaimed even more loudly, "You want the whole of London to think I sew rubbish?" Shaking his head, he stated emphatically, "Absolutely not. I cannot do it! You ask too much!"

It was several moments before they managed to calm the tailor, but they were finally able to reassure him that they were making such an odd request because they were certain they could rely on his discretion. He was the finest tailor in London, they trusted him, and so on – all of which was true. Eventually he was persuaded of their good will, and soon settled enough that they could explain their need.

After more hesitation, the tailor finally nodded and suggested, "I have one idea, but I insist on something from you. When you wear this appalling costume that I provide – against my better judgment – you will *not* mention this establishment, to anyone! It must never be said that Meller would contribute in any way to dressing a man in less than the best fabric, style, quality of work, and fit." The poor man was in a state, but he was fond of Fred and truly wanted to help, so he would do as requested, if they would swear to abide by his terms.

Both men swore their fealty, and Mr. Meller located an old suit that had been badly sewn by a very careless apprentice many years earlier. To reaffirm his high standards, Mr. Meller informed them that he had suggested to the apprentice that he should find another means of livelihood, such as working on the railroad. The suit was very much out of style, improperly cut and stitched, and did not at all fit Fred's proportions. Having been forgotten in a back room for so long, the suit also hosted a large number of very deep wrinkles. Scrooge thought the suit a bit too clean, but knew he could remedy that detail later on, and the tailor need never know.

In the privacy of a securely locked shop, Fred donned the cast-off clothing and stood before the mirror. Mr. Meller was near to weeping, but Scrooge recognized the uncanny resemblance to the dead man, only lacking the facial stubble that Fred must now begin to grow. As to that, neither of them yet knew exactly how Catherine would react to their plan, but they both knew her well enough that they could be certain she would not try to interfere. She would see the value of what they were doing, and if she were unhappy about anything it might be over the fact that she could not go along!

The clothing was stuffed into a Duffel bag and Mr. Meller reassured them that he definitely did not, under any circumstances, wish to see any of the articles ever again. They should be burned! Scrooge and Fred thanked the tailor profusely and offered to recompense him for the fabric, an idea he rejected outright. Never would it be said that he would take, "even a penny for dressing a man in such a schmatte — to you, a 'rag.'" He did appreciate their thanks, however, and begged them to forget that the incident had ever taken place. He hoped the two of them would never mention it again, even to each other.

Uncle and nephew left the shop and walked a while, considering the extraordinary circumstances of this entire situation, when suddenly Scrooge stopped short next to a cab that was about to take on two passengers. Quickly pulling the tailor's throwaways from the bag, he spread them in the street where they would not only be tread on by all four of the horse's hooves, but would also be in the path of the cab's wheels once they began to move.

"Uncle!", yelped Fred. "What are you doing?" Just then the cabby also barked, "'Ere! Wotcha doin' down there?"

Scrooge waved to the cabby that all was well, and replied to Fred, "I am merely increasing the value of your disguise by decreasing its worth as clothing." The cabby shrugged his shoulders and said to his horse, "Well, Nobby, if it's stompin' they want, you're the one to do it!" With that, he clicked his tongue and Nobby and the cab lumbered heavily over the unfortunate suit.

"I must say," said Fred. "I agree with your ingenuity, but you forget that I am the one who is to don that outfit, and I prefer not to be dressed from the gutters of London."

"You may bathe, my boy. You may bathe once this is over."

"And shave," reminded Fred. This entire enterprise was getting worse by the moment and Uncle Scrooge did not seem at all sympathetic, particularly when he retrieved the garments from the street, held them up and smiled broadly as he said, "Perfect! Now you will look like the real thing." It was an apt statement since Fred was already beginning to feel as though he were the real thing.

CHAPTER SIXTEEN

Walking the Villages

T he plan was to ride the railway to Tring and be met by a hired carriage that would take Scrooge and Fred around the settlements near the canal at Marsworth. They would then return to Tring, where they would spend the night near the railway station and visit more villages the following day, if need be. Both Scrooge and Fred knew it might not matter where they began their search because they could well turn up empty-handed no matter how many villages or hamlets they visited, but it was worth a try and it seemed prudent to apply some logic to their search.

Fred's disguise was near perfect. Not only was his clothing poorly enough, it had been several days since he had shaved, and he looked anything but the successful businessman. Scrooge, Homer, and Norris agreed he had an uncanny resemblance to the corpse, a fact that made him inexplicably uncomfortable. With their strategy and Mr. Meller's disguise came several small decisions that must be made. For one, Scrooge must naturally ride in a first-class rail car, but Fred's disguise would preclude him from doing so. Fred would, instead, ride in third class, which was much less comfortable but had, at least, recently been provided the luxury of a roof over the carriage. Riding separately was too bad because they would be unable to discuss anything until their arrival, and the trip would seem much longer, at least to Fred.

The men stood apart as they waited to board the rail cars at Euston Station. Fred glanced about the platform and caught sight of a business associate who was approaching the first-class carriage. Hoping he had not been recognized, Fred spun around, putting his back to the man. Now what? It wouldn't do to bump into him in Tring and try to explain why he was dressed like a pauper, and riding in anything but first class! Then he realized the fellow and Uncle Scrooge would be sharing the same carriage and would no doubt converse and disembark together. These were the snags he had prayed they would not encounter, but perhaps there was a way. If the man disembarked in Tring, Fred would simply hide in the shadows until Scrooge could somehow separate himself from him, which was precisely what occurred. Fred had no way of knowing that his hiding in dark corners was, itself, a shadow of what was to come as he walked in his new, unknown identity.

Homer had arranged that the hired carriage meet them at the station, and it proved to be a good idea, other than the fact that the driver was unsure of what to do with Fred. Addressing Scrooge, he asked, "Are you with this fellow, here?" Scrooge answered in the affirmative, which led the driver to ask, "Are you certain you want to ride together?"

"We do," replied Scrooge, enjoying the game of explaining nothing and observing the driver's attitude. The driver did not speak to Fred once, getting directions from and making comments only to Scrooge. He did not at all wish to be seen driving Fred, but he had no choice, so, wherever possible, he took the less-traveled lanes.

The first settlement they visited was the furthest from the canal locks, and was small and fairly quiet. Scrooge instructed the driver to put them down away from the village, which pleased the driver no end, and to retrieve them within two hours at the same spot. That might raise fewer questions, and the two of them could walk into the settlement separately. It was to be one of their best ideas since it would remove any protection Scrooge's presence might offer Fred, and could, perhaps, garner them a little additional information. What the populace might notice about Fred they might also be willing to share with a gentleman like Scrooge, if they did not suspect they were connected in any way.

Fred lead the way and Scrooge followed at a distance. Walking behind him gave Scrooge an unexpected lesson in poverty and the condition of being an outcast. It was easy to observe what he might miss on the busy streets of London, particularly if he were not familiar with the people and their circumstances. As he followed Fred he noted how passers-by reacted to him. One woman hurriedly ushered her young children across the street before they could encounter the raggedy fellow. A man carrying a large picture frame spat at Fred's feet just as they passed each other, and three young boys ran in a quick circle around him as they chanted, "Cat on a rat . . . bag . . . rat-bag!" The man who had spat at Fred then passed Scrooge, nodded to him and said, "Good day."

In direct contrast to their treatment of Fred, men touched the brims of their hats and the women gave a slight nod to Scrooge, who appeared to be such a gentleman. Scrooge was honest enough with himself to admit that he felt more pity for Fred than he would have felt for someone with whom he was unacquainted. It was a lesson he intended to remember.

Up the street to the small center of things ambled Fred. When he wasn't invisible to the townspeople he was treated with disdain, but no one seemed to recognize him. Having passed a fruiterer, a thought occurred to him. He looked the part, but would his disguise stand, were he to use his usual speech? He was definitely not looking to arouse suspicion, so, without any preparation or practice, he approached the nearest person and enquired the way to the post office, if one existed. He did not sound like himself, at all.

"Do ya 'ave a post office 'round 'ere, then?"

The man looked him up and down, unsure he even wanted to reply to him, and said, "What would you be wanting at a post office, eh? You surely don't have money for a stamp, and I'll wager you don't have mail waiting for you, neither!" Laughing, and without giving Fred an answer to his question, the man continued on his way as if he had just made a very clever joke. Fred was not disappointed, however, since the fellow had just confirmed that his disguise was fairly accurate.

Scrooge, however, was less than pleased as he saw his wonderful nephew being mistreated by people of lesser character.

To further practice and test his speech, Fred turned back and approached the fruiterer, who was arranging a small outdoor display. With a tone of humility he asked, "You wouldn't 'ave a bit of food fer an 'ungry unfortunate now, would ya?" The shopkeeper was of a kindly nature and handed Fred a handful of his best cherries, with the admonition that he be sure to enjoy them. How Fred wished he could pay the man more than his humble thanks, but he needn't have concerned himself because Scrooge, following behind, saw the transaction and handed the man much more than the cherries were worth. "I'll pay for his fruit," said Scrooge, "and may God bless you for your generous nature."

It was not difficult to locate what served as a tiny post office, and Fred stood at the entry, simply to see if anyone recognized him. He looked inside a bit, ignoring the stares from the postmaster and the one patron, remaining only until the postmaster ordered him to remove himself if he had no business to conduct. Fred gave an acquiescent nod before he turned aside and sat down, leaning his back against the outside of the building. He was in place just before Scrooge strode by. Since no one could hear him, Scrooge said, "I think we will amble by the forge. Blacksmiths always know most of what's going on."

The forge was not far, and Scrooge approached first. "Good day," said he to the smith. "I am traveling through and I wonder, how long would it take you to replace a shoe on a horse?" It was not a lie, it was simply a request for information. The smith held off striking some red-hot metal and said, "Well now, I could most likely do it in less time than it would take you to walk where you're goin', that's for sure!" Laughing, he suggested that Scrooge bring the horse to him, and he would have a look at it.

Pointing to Fred, who was ambling toward them, Scrooge asked, "Is he one of your help?"

The smith frowned and shook his head. "Never seen him b'fore, and I can tell he in't from 'round here, 'cause I know ever'body." Then he gave Fred a good look-over and pronounced, "Nah, he don' belong in these parts, poor beggar."

The smith no doubt did know everyone in the village, so Scrooge thanked him and began walking in the direction of where they were to meet the hired carriage. He was, of course, followed by Fred, who used a circuitous route and kept a good distance between them. They spent the night at an inn near the rail line, where Fred was able to change back into his normal clothes and once again become himself, other than his stubble of beard. Something within him had been altered by the experience, however.

Over supper, Fred admitted that he had been surprised at how quickly one could be humbled by how he was dressed, and how he spoke. Having just enjoyed a fine piece of beef, he said, "It seems to affect a person's very character, and I am convinced it makes even the idea of success a difficult thing to imagine." Scrooge was watching him as if waiting for him to say more, so he did.

"It didn't take long for me to sense that I was actually beneath others, and it was a very uncomfortable experience. Instead of simply telling people what I wanted or needed, I found myself entreating them, asking for favors and pleading with them to kindly lower themselves to help me." He leaned back and concluded with, "It was quite an eye-opener, I can tell you, and I will never again assume that the fellow who has less than I should be able to easily conjure up enough gumption to posthaste pull himself out of the gutter! There are times, I am certain, when a little help can go a long way."

As he thought back on the day, Fred suddenly smiled and wished the good fruiterer happiness as he admitted, "I reck'n, Uncle, them cherries may 'a been th' best I ever 'ad, n' they was free, too!" Scrooge chuckled and replied, "Yes, my boy, they were free — to you."

⊂ଓଃଓ

As arranged, the following morning the driver reappeared to take them to the second village in their plan. The poor man was finding it difficult not to expose his curiosity and had worried himself all night. He had to ask, "How is it you two know each other, and what brings you to these parts?"

Scrooge was ready for him, and replied, "We have a connection through my father (which was true since Scrooge's father was Fred's grandfather) and I am assisting this fellow in identifying someone he has never seen." That was also true since Fred had not seen the body in the barge. It sounded very much like a riddle, but it was enough to stave off further questions from the driver. He realized he would get nothing meaningful from them, so he simply said, "Walk on" to the horse, and they went their way to the second village on the list.

This settlement was closer in proximity to the locks and there was more activity in the streets, with more houses, shops, and taverns. Its larger population meant not only more hustle, but surely more problems, which may very well have included the man whose identity they sought. Scrooge and Fred supposed their unknown unfortunate had been a troubled fellow and may have been considered a bane to at least one person in the village. His having been secretively stowed onto a barge and sent to an unknown destination was evidence that such might be the case. There could be little doubt that a secret of some sort was behind the act.

Repeating their previous day's routine, the driver let the men out on the outskirts of the village and once again Scrooge followed behind Fred. The driver observed them, shaking his head as if he had just realized he was dealing with at least one parolee from Bedlam, and he'd best be wary of mishandling them. It wouldn't do to be set upon by a madman and his keeper, particularly on a less traveled lane!

Fred was still surprised by how simply wearing dirty cast-off clothing and altering his speech could result in such a change in his opinion of himself. He would not have realized, otherwise, how a good suit of clothes or the proper choice of words enhanced one's confidence. Certainly, he would have agreed, had someone said that was the case, but now he "knew" it from his own experience, and he commenced his charade with a fairly convincing attitude.

Up the High Street they walked, with Fred meandering about some of the shop windows, peering in until he caught the proprietor's eye before moving on. He dawdled too long at one shop and was forthwith chased away by an owner who yelled some very unkind things. It was an experience he never wished to repeat. He then loitered on the green for a bit, sitting on a large stone. He was unsure whether or not to smile at passers-by, so he tried various expressions, none of which affected a pleasantry in return. In fact, most of their faces reflected pure hatred and distrust. Sometimes, fear and surprise.

Neither Fred nor Scrooge noticed that several children were peeking at Fred from the corner of a building as if plotting their attack, which is exactly what came next. Without warning, Fred was assailed with what had once been a fruit or a vegetable but was nothing but rotted mush by the time it hit Fred. The foray was short-lived because the children scattered when Fred leapt up and lashed back with terrible threats. He had done so before he realized it, and was surprised and disappointed that he could host such violence in his heart. But then, he had never before been the object of this sort of thing, had he?

There were other eyes observing him, and his most recent action caused a stir. Had he been able to listen in he would have heard snippets such as, "Did you see?" "Oh, it's him, alright . . ." "His stride is unlike . . ." "See for yourself . . ." People scurried back and forth, trying not to be caught out, marveling at what they believed was playing out before their very eyes.

Fred meandered on down the street, and Scrooge took notice of all that occurred. He had been tempted to rescue Fred but knew that would only curtail their efforts. It was unlikely that their unknown unfortunate would have had a well-to-do benefactor following him about, protecting him. Therefore, Scrooge kept his distance.

It became evident that they were nearing success when a woman saw Fred, let out a small squeal, and promptly fainted. Her friends picked her up, all of them wide-eyed, and ushered her away as one fanned her face. When Scrooge passed by, he inquired, "What has occurred?", and was told, indicating Fred, "That man . . . he's . . ." as the women hurried away.

Fred was growing weary and found himself at the doorway of The Bald Parrot, a local pub, so he slipped in to sit a while and have a swallow of something. He could always ask Scrooge to pay for it by pretending he was begging from a kind-hearted stranger.

There was a good bit of racket coming from within, with an active darts game and jovial bantering among several men. All of that ceased, however, a moment after Fred stepped in and his presence was noted by the men, one by one. He stood for a moment, assessing the interior and its occupants while he searched for a place to sit. As he did so, he realized all of the noise in the place had died down to a total silence. It was absolutely still. No one moved, including the man ready to throw the winning dart. Everyone stared at Fred, their eyes wide. The only thing that moved was the ale the bartender was over-pouring, since he was no longer paying a bit of attention to the fact that he was doing so. He, and everyone else, was concentrating, instead, on the apparition standing before him.

Scrooge had followed Fred inside and saw it all, later recalling that it was as if, upon seeing Fred, the group had unwittingly positioned themselves in a tableau — one that could be titled "The Second Coming in The Bald Parrot."

In the eerie silence, Scrooge joined Fred from behind and murmured, "My boy, it looks as if we may have found your identity. Now, if we can just give you a name!" That was forthcoming, when the man holding the dart cried, "Hugh Weld!" Addressing the other men in a lowered voice, he asked, "'Ow's 'e 'ere, then? 'E's dead! Ain't 'e dead?", and the other men agreed, creating an altogether new din, with everyone talking at once. Then the noise died again since no one knew what to say, once they had expressed their initial shock.

Seizing the opportunity, Fred replied, "Dead 'n laid in a boat. Still, I'm standin' 'ere now, ain't I?" The dart player approached him warily, as if Fred might spring on him at any moment, and walked half-way around him, examining. He said to the others, "It's gotta be 'im, awright. Only it in't possible, 'cause we all seen him an' 'e was deader'n a door stop, 'e were." With that, the men slowly began to scrutinize Fred from a distance and with a good deal of trepidation. "It's revenge, that's wot it is!", whimpered a man from somewhere in the group. Another one echoed that sentiment with, "It's retaliation, awright, but we wasn't to blame!", and they all joined the chorus by agreeing, "That's right. It weren't our fault!"

Neither Fred nor Scrooge had planned what to do should Fred be recognized, so they did the first thing that came to mind. Hoping to get some answers, Fred asked, with a bit of a threat to his voice, "And jus' wot about me is so terrifyin?" The very question resulted in the men's backing away. All would have sworn that he was no longer among the living, and they could not account for him standing there unless they were being haunted by his ghost – one who had the appearance of being very real, at that.

Before they could reply to Fred, however, a tumult arose outside. The villagers had quickly alerted each other to the fact that Hugh Weld had been loosed from the grave and was strolling about. Whether he be flesh or spirit, they were having none of it. They were not even able to agree on whether or not it truly was Weld, but that didn't matter. A menace was a menace, and the resemblance was close enough that he must be got rid of! Men had grabbed anything handy that might be used as a club, and the women were encouraging them to put an end to the threat. Amid the general uproar could be heard the occasional, ". . . gone once't an' fer all!", and ". . . away from here!" There was evidently not one person in town who was glad to see the return of Hugh Weld, nor anyone closely favoring him. To be precise, Fred Symons was about to be run out of town on another man's reputation!

Scrooge sprang into action and slammed and secured the tavern door, further barring it with his body while Fred resorted to his normal and more proper speech. It gave them enough time to approach the tavern patrons with their very unusual situation.

Fred quickly began. "Men, I am not a ghost, as you can well discern. I am a man like yourselves, but I happen to resemble someone you call Weld. He is, as you say, dead and buried by my family, who believed him to be me. We need to know who he is, because surely someone is mourning him and needs to know how and where he died. His family has a need to know where he is buried." This remark garnered several derisive snorts from the men, but at the least they were placated, and no longer afraid.

It was enough to calm the interior of the tavern, but the folks outside were still in an uproar. The tavern owner edged Scrooge away from the door, opened it and barked, "'Ere, you got the wrong end of the stick! This bloke's not dead, an' 'es not Weld, so go on 'ome an' stop all of this commotion! We'll take care of it in 'ere. Go on 'ome, now." As they drifted away, murmuring to themselves, the proprietor returned to his station, poured two brews and set them before Scrooge and Fred.

The man who was still holding the dart finally set it down and began. "It's uncanny, that's wot it is. You could be that good-fer-nuthin sot, for sure – leastwise, until you speak the King's English." With that, there were several small chuckles, and the group settled down. Two more had entered the assembly after the villagers were dispersed; the schoolmaster, whose students had rushed out of the school to join their parents in the melee; and the vicar. Both were able and willing to lend their knowledge to the discussion.

After introductions, the vicar began. "Mr. Symons, I have never seen anything like this in my life, and I am sorry you found yourself in this situation, but as you can see, your look-alike was not well thought of in these parts." Realizing he had not quite spoken the truth, he added, "No, the fact is, he was very much despised," and the schoolmaster, as well as everyone in the tavern, nodded in agreement. Some added their comments, such as, "'E were a bad 'un, that's for sure," and, "We was that glad to see 'im gone fer good, 'n then you showed up." Another man ventured to say, "We been fearin' someone might come after us, but not 'is ghost — walking right in 'ere, to haunt us!"

That was the opening Scrooge needed, so he asked, "Why would you think someone would come after you?", but he received nothing but stubborn silence. No one wanted to admit anything until the schoolmaster urged, "Come now, men, you might as well be out with it, rather than live in fear of something similar to what has occurred today, where you might even be called to account by someone with more authority." His remark was met with more subdued murmurings, but eventually it became obvious that the group was in agreement to tell the story, but who should tell it? The man with the winning dart, who had played such a large part in the event? Or perhaps the tavern keeper, who witnessed everything the most clearly? Or should it be the older man with the cane, over whom the incident began? Nor should the rest of the men be discounted, since each had played his small part, in the end.

Perhaps it was best if the victor appointed each one to simply tell his portion of the incident. So, he began with Old Duncan, the man with the cane. "Come now, Duncan, you may as well tell these good men how it all began. I would say they have a right to know, and they don't seem to be out for blood."

Duncan was overtaken by shallow coughs before he could speak, and the bartender handed him half a pint. He took a long swallow, then began. "Well," he rasped, "I was sittin' here, right where I am now, when that slugabed wandered in. "He were lookin' fer trouble, which weren't anythin' new, but this time he were fightin' mad, with fire in 'is eyes, 'n he were seekin' a way to start a row." Thumping his cane on the floor as he recalled the humiliating indignity of it all, he said, "Everbody ignored him, which was hard to do, so he looks straight at me 'n says, 'You! Old Duncan! Wot you lookin' at?" He didn' want answerin', he jus' wanted to pick a fight, even with somebody like me, who couldn't fight back 'cause I'm all crippled up." Suddenly Duncan began another coughing fit and the men grumbled again, reliving their anger over Weld's treatment of a sorry old man. Duncan attempted to continue, but was interrupted by Cecil, the barman, who took up the story.

"Duncan jus' looks at him 'n didn't answer, so Weld grabs him 'n tosses him like a rag doll against that table over there. I thought sure he'd cracked up some of those brittle bones of his, 'n I thought, 'Well now, that's done it, but at least Weld will leave 'n we'll patch up Old Duncan and get him home,' but Weld hadn't spent all of his rage yet. He picked up Duncan's cane and started in beatin' him with it . . ." At that point, Cecil was interrupted by Simon, the man with the dart.

"We all saw what was 'appenin', 'n somthin' popped inside me. I jus' grabbed Weld, spun 'im 'round and knocked 'im to the floor. So 'elp me, I woulda killed 'im if these blokes 'ere hadn't pulled me off 'im. I was that done with the man." Another voice broke in and cried, "We'd put up with 'im for years now, 'n even our wives 'n daughters were pestered by 'im on the streets!" Someone else said, "It all come to an 'ead, right then." One man admitted their intentions by saying, "We'd pulled Simon off 'im, but we was all gettin' ready to give 'im ever' one of our fists, an' the blows of our boots, too!" Finally, someone summed things up with, "We was ready to be finished with 'im an' 'is behavior fer good, an' that's a fact!"

Simon continued. "As they was pullin' me offa 'im I readied m'self to pounce on 'im again, 'cause I planned to finish the job right there 'n then, but I needn't 'a worried 'cause destiny did the job for me. I'd pulled 'im back onto 'is feet 'n reared back to give 'im the thrashin' 'e needed when, of a sudden, th' cursed man stood stiff as a board. 'E jus' stood there an' got this blank look about 'im. It was like 'e weren't seein' nuthin', 'n then 'e jus keeled over, right there where young Tom's standin'. 'E never said a word. 'E jus' hit the floor 'n laid there like 'e'd been taken by surprise — sorta like 'is spirit 'ad jumped right outta 'is body 'n left it to slam onto the floor, empty like."

Cecil, the barman, picked up the tale from there. "We checked him 'n he was dead, alright; deader'n a Christmas goose, 'n good riddance. I mean, he just up 'n died right on the spot, but it wasn't anybody's doing. Nobody'd laid a finger on him, except Simon, 'n he hadn't yet give him more'n a blinker an' maybe a busted lip; sure not 'nuff to make him depart this world." Simon nodded and said, "But we was scared 'cause we surely was ready t' kill 'im, even though we didn't. We knew we could be blamed for it, but we didn' know what to do, jus' then. 'Bout the only thing goin' for us was the fact that not one person 'oo knew 'im liked 'im. There wouldn't be nobody who'd try to get the law on us, but we still didn' want t' chance it."

The barman then said, "So we had to find a way to get rid of th' body. We all figured if he just disappeared no one would care, much less try to find out why, or how. Fact is, they would all be more'n glad about it, 'n most likely wouldn't ask no questions. Word did get about, of course, 'n everbody heard he was dead, but they kept their mouths shut to outsiders, and to the one or two of the locals what might spread the word where they shouldn't."

"We stuck 'im in the old larder out back until we could decide wot to do," said Simon. "'E were layin' in there a couple of days 'n then someone ('oo I won't name) copped some dirty ice from somewhere's 'n packed 'im in it for another two or three days. 'Bout that time somebody – I think it was George, over there – got the idea to put 'im on a passin' barge. We give a local dipper a few coins to arrange to stow 'im in one goin' south 'n thought that would be th' last of it, 'cuz somebody at th' end of the line would deal with the body." Addressing Scrooge, he said, "Turns out it was you wot did the disposin' for us, thinkin' it was this 'ere gent," pointing toward Fred.

"It's the God's truth, that's wot happened, an' we ain't apologizin' for it," said the barkeeper, and there was a general buzz of agreement from the crowd.

The schoolmaster had not yet said spoken, but believed it was necessary to complete the picture of Weld. He began by addressing both Scrooge and Fred. "Gentlemen, lest you think we are a community of barbarians, I must tell you that every description of Hugh Weld is true, and everyone in the village who might be aware of the event of that evening knows that this tale of his demise is also true. I can verify the character of Weld, who was not a victim of murder, nor even manslaughter. He was a victim of his own fallen nature and he was a true misery to those who had the misfortune of coming into contact with him. He was a thief, a liar, and a bully. He had injured more than one person and threatened many others. His character was volatile, and if I had to wager, I'd say he died of apoplexy."

To further verify his statements, the schoolmaster added, "I taught Hugh in lower grades, before he stopped attending school altogether, and he had not one friend since he knew only how to be an enemy. It was sad, but he would not be turned around because he refused to respond to kindness – other than from animals, that is, particularly his dog. When he received gentleness from people he always returned abuse. I believe he was clever and bright, but he was not astute enough to see the damage he did to himself, and to others, nor did he seem to care. He could never be brought to the point of redemption because he never admitted the need. At one time I suspected the problem was that he believed he was 'too far gone' to change, but neither I, nor the Vicar, was ever able to pierce the deep darkness that engulfed him."

Both Scrooge and Fred sat still, having nothing further to ask. It was clear that Fred's look-alike did not resemble Fred in any way but countenance, and it was difficult to know whether they should feel pity, or loathing, for the man. Scrooge tended toward disdain, but Fred, having just been through what it was like to "be" Hugh Weld, was a little less certain. Then Scrooge did think of the last important question.

"His family . . ." began Scrooge and was met with laughter and hoots of disgust. The reaction of the group shocked him, and just as he was about to enquire regarding their reaction, the bartender explained.

"He only had his mum, 'n she's not much better'n him. Fact is, we don' know if she's been told what happened, or not, 'n no one really cares, if you take my meaning. She don't mix much 'n nobody goes to see 'er. I'd wager a sovereign that not one villager would bother to make the trip to inform her, leastwise not unless they was paid to do it. Even then they'd most likely jus' shout the information out at her, from a distance!"

Scrooge did take his meaning, but still felt a responsibility to deal with her since they had claimed and buried the body of her son, no matter how insufferable he may have been. So, he obtained her name and direction from the schoolmaster and he and Fred departed the tavern with various expressions of good luck ringing in their ears. They had much to discuss and should make no more decisions without first consulting Rollo Norris, which they would do upon their return to London.

Poor Fred continued to receive suspicious glares from a few of the more superstitious villagers, and one or two insults were tossed his way in a futile attempt to have the last word with Hugh Weld. At least he and Scrooge now knew the identity of the corpse, and both of them believed the tale of how he had died. There certainly had been a sufficient number of witnesses to verify the fact.

The driver and his carriage were waiting for them, still with a bit of trepidation, but Fred was now used to causing such a reaction. He easily entered the carriage for the ride back to the inn, where he could at last wash, shave and change back into his own clothes, for good. Over the course of two days the driver had not spoken one word to him, and the few words Fred had uttered in his presence were in less than perfect English.

On the train back to London, Fred, who once again resembled a first-class passenger, remarked, "Uncle, I do not wish to complain, but before we entertain a conversation about our adventures, I might mention that I have brought on a screaming fit in my wife, who was terrified by my appearance; received a battering by an umbrella; been insulted and bombarded with rotten produce; caused a near riot, and brought on at least two fits of fainting."

Suddenly recalling one more thing, he held up his index finger and added, "Oh, yes! And I have even begged for my food!" His statement was somewhat humorous to them both, but he wanted to make a point. "I only wish you to take that into consideration when we discuss this affair. I do not require sympathy, but I definitely seek understanding should we find ourselves in opposing positions on this matter. I pray we won't, but if it should be so, please have patience." Scrooge smiled and said he understood, but he did not expect them to be at odds over anything they had discovered.

Scrooge had also been doing some thinking and said, offhandedly, "I believe, in future, we should consider brokering more shipments via the railways, rather than the canals. What say you?", and they both smiled wearily as they sat back in their seats to let the steam engine pull them home.

CHAPTER SEVENTEEN

Mrs. Lucy Pearce, Martha Cratchit and Rose

Bob Cratchit's oldest child, Martha, had been employed by the widowed milliner Lucy Pearce for well over two years now, and Mr. and Mrs. Cratchit were vastly proud of her and her situation. They held Mrs. Pearce in high esteem and did not worry about Martha as she served under her supervision.

Martha had secured the situation because of her previous employment as a seamstress with knowledge of textiles, and also because her appearance and demeanor suggested she was of a class well above the circumstances of her birth. Mrs. Pearce had taken to her immediately, as did all of her customers. Martha would never mislead a woman, no matter her age, into thinking she could wear something that was not becoming, but she could tell the truth about what was appropriate without belittling, and certainly without giving insult. Martha was also very creative. She designed millinery that rivaled the best London had to offer, for which Mrs. Pearce could then charge a good price, and for which Martha was well-paid. In addition, she was rewarded by Mrs. Pearce's true friendship. After all, the difference in age was not so very great, if one actually totaled the years.

Employer and employee spent many hours in each other's company, so they naturally fell to discussing more than simply changing fashions and how to trim a bonnet. At times they spoke of more personal subjects, sharing their thoughts and sentiments concerning their personal lives. Although she did not realize it at the time, Martha invariably shared a great deal about herself, while her employer shared much less. Martha knew that Mrs. Pearce was a widow, but she knew little else.

Having established a friendly intimacy, it naturally followed that Martha would speak of romance. Mrs. Pearce offered nothing from her own experiences and Martha took no notice because she was too preoccupied with the subject of Homer and Rollo. Both men were quite taken with Martha and made no secret of it, which had managed to confuse her, all the while making her heart flutter. She found both men attractive and she had earlier believed she and Homer might someday make a match, although Rollo's attentions had introduced some doubt as to that.

Martha was not full of tittle-tattle because she was more serious-minded than that, and she was certainly not silly, but the nearest she ever came to being missish was in discussion of her suitors. "Both are handsome," she once admitted to Mrs. Pearce, "but they are not at all alike. Homer is steady and more gentleman-like. Rollo can seem somewhat brash, but I'm certain his character is good. He simply has a disparate way of showing it." Tilting her head, she mused, "I suppose, in all fairness, that may be owing to the fact that he is a policeman, don't you agree?"

Mrs. Pearce was not always required to reply to Martha's comments because hers was a busy shop and they were often interrupted, at least during hours of operation. So, these discussions could take place over a period of hours, or days, and eventually Mrs. Pearce was able to put together a fairly accurate picture of the two men and their effects on Martha. It seemed to Mrs. Pearce that both truly cared for her but, for some reason, Mrs. Pearce trusted Homer the more.

Mrs. Pearce was remarkably proficient at her occupation. Through the years she had acquired a clear understanding of her trade, and commerce in general. She also possessed the talent required to provide a quality product to her patrons, but she realized that talent, alone, did not dictate success. Many extremely talented individuals in London had not succeeded simply because, in truth, they were not effective in their dealings with others. So, at the outset she had determined that she would treat her patrons with respect and deference, all the while providing excellent merchandise. It was not difficult for her since she did have an aptitude for fashion and a humble kindness that put people at ease. Her philosophy and its resultant success had been severely endangered on only one occasion.

Because the shop could be very busy, another employee, Rose, was engaged to assist. She was a bit younger than Martha and had little of Martha's poise and ability, but she was presentable, reasonably intelligent and steady, and earned her pay. Mrs. Pearce came to learn, however, that Rose was best put to use stocking materials and keeping the place clean and organized, rather than serving the ladies who entered the shop. That decision came as a result of Rose's first encounter with a regular patron, at a time when she was still new to her situation and had not the skills required to bring about a satisfactory transaction. In fact, she was simply not suited, and the problem came to light most painfully with poor Mrs. Bell.

Mrs. Bell, whose name very much resembled the shape of her face, entered the shop one day, settled heavily into her usual chair in front of her usual mirror, expecting the usual service. Instead, Rose approached her and asked if she could be of assistance.

"No, young lady, you may not. I do not know you and I prefer to be helped by either Mrs. Pearce, or Miss Cratchit." Neither was available, and since Rose did not want to fail in her first attempt, she persisted, rather than fetch one of them.

"I am certain I can give satisfactory service, ma'am, if you will just tell me what it is you wish to see."

"A hat, of course, my girl. I am in need of a hat. You are aware that headgear is created and sold here, are you not?" Giving her an examining stare, Mrs. Bell asked, "Who are you?"

"My name is Rose, Ma'am," and although Mrs. Bell had not yet given Rose permission to serve her, Rose pressed on, certain she could please her. Yes, she would sell her a very nice item and be rewarded by satisfying her employer!

Without prelude, and giving Mrs. Bell no opportunity to resist, Rose began to remove Mrs. Bell's bonnet. Since she was not adept at removing anything from someone else's head, the unfortunate result was that the bonnet caught Mrs. Bell's hair. Rose had also neglected to untie the ribbon from under Mrs. Bell's several chins, and it all became a tangle in which a handful of Mrs. Bell's hair came undone, falling over her face. The bonnet was now dangling from her neck, but Rose somehow managed to yank the ribbon and release the thing, allowing it to fall to the floor. Poor Rose wanted to repair the damage she had caused, but all she knew to do was wad Mrs. Bell's loose hair into a ball and place it back atop her head.

"Here, girl! Watch what you are about!", cried Mrs. Bell. "What's happening? Ack! I'm coming undone!"

Unfortunately, Rose had not planned how to hold the knob in place. Doing as best she could, with her left hand she held the wadded mass in place, and with her right hand she removed two hairpins from elsewhere on Mrs. Bell's head. Naturally, the result was a sudden release of even more hair, which caused Rose to let go the wad she was holding. It happened so quickly that Mrs. Bell managed to react only as her coiffure had been absolutely torn apart.

"Oh! Stupid girl! What do you think you are about? Look what you've done! It took my maid an hour to fashion my hair this morning and you have torn it to shreds in half a minute! Oh, this is beyond anything!"

Rose felt as undone as Mrs. Bell's hairstyle, and in her alarm, she became desperate to succeed. Grabbing a new hat, Rose clumsily banged it down on Mrs. Bell's head, somewhat askew, and quickly remarked what a lovely thing it was, although Mrs. Bell was not quite able to see it because of the hair that was in her eyes. For a reason Rose could not explain at the time, nor ever after, she tried to right the hat and secure it using a nearby hat pin, which she grabbed and promptly stuck into the bonnet — a bit too far.

"Ow! Help! Ooooh! What are you doing girl, trying to kill me?" Bending toward the mirror, Mrs. Bell parted the hair from her face, attempted to examine her scalp in the reflection, and cried, "Blood! I'm sure I'm bleeding! Will someone please help me? I've been punctured by this madwoman! Eeeeek!"

The commotion finally reached Mrs. Pearce and she came running from the back room, where she had been keeping books. She quickly surveyed the scene before her, shooed Rose out of the way, and examined Mrs. Bell's head. There was a small pin prick, but no amount of blood. Her physical injury was not equal to her reaction, although the assault on her pride certainly had been. It was imperative that Mrs. Pearce use her skills, and act immediately. Even had Mrs. Bell not been a valued customer, Mrs. Pearce would have patted and calmed her, which she did, taking the time to repair her coiffure. She would do what she must, to make amends.

As Mrs. Pearce skillfully repaired the intricate coiffure, she said, "My dear Mrs. Bell, I cannot apologize enough, to make up for what has occurred. Please allow me to fetch you a cup of tea, and we will sit a while." Since entering the shop Mrs. Bell had been treated to an extreme amount of attention, much of it abominable, but the solicitous ministrations of Mrs. Pearce eventually placated her.

"Mrs. Pearce," cried Mrs. Bell, "I cannot deny it. That young woman has very nearly cost you a cherished patron, if I may consider myself such." With a softer tone, she added, "On the other hand, you are the best milliner I have found, and I would not like to embark on a search for someone else who might, or might not, serve me so well as you."

Mrs. Pearce breathed a silent "thank You" to heaven, then uttered her gratitude to Mrs. Bell, concluding with, "I sincerely pray you will forgive us this morning's unfortunate episode. I consider it a merciful act on your part that you could manage to overlook the mistakes of a young, enthusiastic employee and allow us to continue to serve you in future."

Not yet willing to release her newfound power, Mrs. Bell preened somewhat, sucked her teeth and replied, "Ah, well now, that is the thing, isn't it? I will certainly return *if* you can guarantee that your wild young mischief-maker will never come near me again!" Anxious to use the unfortunate occurrence to even more advantage, Mrs. Bell continued. "I have never been so mistreated by anyone in trade, and I must confess that I believe I truly should seek another milliner, but as I said, I will give you another chance." With that, Mrs. Bell suggested that a new hat, at no cost to her, would be most appreciated, and Mrs. Pearce quickly agreed. Much later, as a mollified Mrs. Bell finally departed the shop, Mrs. Pearce collapsed into the nearest chair and let out a long, relieved sigh. She would rest a bit before speaking with Rose.

Rose was eventually located cowering in a corner near the back of the building, which was what had often worked when she needed to avoid the rage of a drunken father. So, it was natural that she expected at least a stern scolding, if not a slap or two, to be followed by outright dismissal. She stood stock still, facing Mrs. Pearce, and hung her head, ashamed and waiting for the dressing-down and the blows. Instead, Mrs. Pearce spoke with a note of sympathy in her voice.

"You were not entirely at fault, Rose. I should not have left you alone in the shop, and I should have at least advised you to call me if a patron entered the premises. Now, in future, I will require at least two things from you. You are not to deal directly with anyone unless I ask you to, and you do not perform any tasks unless I have previously taught you how to do so. Is that clear?"

Yes, it surely was! Rose looked up with adoration in her eyes and nodded energetically. She heard most of what Mrs. Pearce had just said but was so overjoyed at the leniency she had been granted that she was much too overcome to speak. Even though she had been struck dumb in her gratefulness, her thoughts were racing. Mrs. Pearce was the kindest, gentlest, best employer in the whole of London, and that was the truth! Rose would serve her until her dying days, she was certain of it!

CHAPTER EIGHTEEN

Lost Love

Today Martha Cratchit was away from the shop, making a personal delivery of a new bonnet, Rose was running an errand, and Mrs. Pearce was left alone in the shop. She was adorning a hat with ribbon when she heard the door slowly open. She turned with a smile and offered a polite "May I assist you?" to the man standing just inside. He had removed his hat but remained where he was, his expression a mixture of pleasure and apprehension.

Mrs. Pearce repeated her question, thinking he had not heard. "May I assist you, Sir? Are you seeking something for your wife?" He seemed pleasant enough, but it was not uncommon for men who found themselves in feminine settings to suddenly fall mute.

"Lucy," he said, simply, as if he couldn't believe his eyes. "You haven't changed a bit, and I thought I hadn't either, but I see that I have by the fact that you no longer recognize me." What had been a detached awareness turned to scrutiny as Mrs. Pearce studied his countenance more closely, and he helped her to recollect. "There was a time, I'd wager, that you would have known me from a distance, and even tried to close that distance quickly. Do you recall how you used to slip your arm in mine and walk with me on a Sunday afternoon? Don't you really know me, my girl?"

Of course, she knew him! Lucy dropped her ribbon, covered her mouth with her hand and asked, timidly, "Edwin? Edwin Carter? Can it really be you?" Could this truly be the man on whom she had once pinned all of her hopes, only to have them collapse with his sailing to America? All of his attempts to better himself in England had resulted in failure, but she believed in him then, and did yet. Mrs. Pearce knew he would succeed in America, but at this point she never expected to see him again. She had tried to make a life for herself as best she could, and had done very well, at that.

Her heart was beating beyond what she thought it capable. *What does he want with me now? He looks well enough and is certainly as fine a figure as ever he was, but what can his reappearance mean?*

"I see that you are married, Lucy. You're now a missus, but I don't recognize the surname. Given that you've a husband, I hope you will forgive my intrusion into your day, but I could not return to London without seeing you again and ensuring that all is well with you."

With a great deal of effort Mrs. Pearce maintained the appearance of composure and asked, "How did you locate me, Edwin, since you knew me only by my maiden name of Edgar?"

"I did a bit of detection, my dear. I spoke with your old employers, after some weeks of re-discovering their names and ferreting out their current whereabouts. One of them, a Mrs. Holding, told me she had sought you out several years ago, curious as to whether a milliner by the name of Lucy Pearce might be her old employee, and that you were, indeed, Lucy Edgar. She described your lovely shop and gave me its direction, but said she knew nothing of Mr. Pearce." Mr. Carter did a good job of hiding his hope when he asked, "Are you a widow, then?"

Mrs. Pearce did not look at him when she replied, "No, Edwin, I am not a widow."

Mr. Carter's face fell at this news, but he had not traveled thousands of miles to leave without a visit, and he was also determined to make certain she was well cared for because, if she were not, he would make the offer of anything she might require in the way of assistance. "Lucy, please have a cup of tea with me and we can talk through old times a bit, then I will leave you to your new life, which I see is very comfortable."

Mrs. Pearce was about to make the excuse that she could not leave the shop unattended, when Martha hurried through the door. "Please forgive me for taking so long," she cried, somewhat out of breath, "but you know how difficult a home delivery and fitting can be. Mrs. Hardwick finally settled on the hat, and seems very happy . . ." Seeing Mr. Carter standing to the side, she nodded, gave a very slight curtsey and said, "Oh! Please excuse me for interrupting."

Mrs. Pearce extended her hand toward Mr. Carter and said, more calmly than she felt, "Martha Cratchit, may I introduce to you an old acquaintance of mine. This is Mr. Edwin Carter, who has just returned to London after several years away."

Martha's reaction was more than her usual small curtsey and reserved "How do you do?" Instead, she smiled broadly and quickly exclaimed, "Why, yes! You must be the businessman who has just returned from America, are you not? My father has spoken highly of you. He has very much enjoyed making your acquaintance and doing business with you." Realizing she had not given enough information, Martha quickly added, "My father is Mr. Scrooge's clerk, Bob Cratchit."

Mr. Carter's smile was immediate and genuine. "Yes, Martha. I have met your father and I look forward to seeing a great deal more of him in future." Giving a small bow he said, "And now I have also met his charming daughter, of whom I have heard such glowing reports. This is entirely my pleasure, Miss." A man of action, he seized the opportunity and ventured to boldly ask, "Martha, would you consider minding the place while your employer and I have a cup of tea at Twinings? We have much to discuss."

Martha quickly assented, with a gleam in her eye, which Mrs. Pearce caught when the women looked at each other. Yes, this was something, indeed, that they would discuss when Mrs. Pearce returned. At that moment it occurred to Martha that she had never elicited as much information from Mrs. Pearce as she had thought. Come to think on it, she knew next to nothing about her employer!

CƷȢↃ

Once settled at a table, Mr. Carter and Mrs. Pearce fell into an awkward and uncomfortable silence. He was used to taking the lead in situations, being generally undeterred and quite sure of himself, but this was entirely different. They found themselves in a unique position. The two of them had enjoyed a previous acquaintance that was much more than a passing friendship, but their past was so long ago that neither knew what to do with the present.

After ordering tea and biscuits, Mr. Carter began. "Ahem. I realize this is difficult, but perhaps we should begin with history. Are you willing to look back, just for a bit? It might ease our conversation. What do you say?"

Mrs. Pearce had no idea what to say, so she simply nodded her head very slightly, leaving him to begin the conversation with whatever seemed best. While he searched his memories for the best way to begin, she took a sip of tea.

"My Dear, if I may call you that with only respect, I know I have no right to offer more than friendship at this point in your life, and I hope you will forgive me for acting in a very ungentlemanly way, but there is something I must say, and then be done with it. *Why should this be so difficult? It isn't solely that she is married to some other, very fortunate man. It is that I need to explain my actions since they must have appeared to her to be abjectly remiss. Although it is far too late to be saying them, now that we are together, I must at least try.*

"When I left several years ago I did not forfeit our plans for the future, although I do admit it took me much longer than I expected. In addition, lest you believe me fickle, I swear now that I wrote several letters, which I assume you either did not receive, or could not answer due to being married. I am not blaming you for marrying because no woman should be expected to wait for a suitor who leaves the country and is gone for nearly a decade, no matter their mutual regard, or the promises they may have whispered by candlelight." His heart was aching, but he forced himself to continue.

"I must, however, state what may not be apparent, although I suspect it is. Please forgive me for saying this, but I adored you then and my feelings have not changed. You see, I have been absent, but not inconstant. My sole purpose in returning to England was to find you. I could have remained in America and lived a comfortable life, but once I had succeeded, there was nothing there for me. I wanted to see you once more because I still had hopes, you understand, and I am so sorry that it was my doing that made us part."

Poor Mrs. Pearce was now in a state of visible upset, and Mr. Carter was fearful for her. Without thinking, he took her hand to calm her and she gave way to the huge tears that had been brimming for several moments. As they slid down her cheeks he thought, *Oh, what an idiot I am! The last thing I wished was to distress this splendid woman.* He was beside himself. What had he done? What should he do? He was on the verge of asking for assistance from someone when Mrs. Pearce seemed to rally and began to speak. Her voice was weak at first, but as she related certain facts she gained more confidence and found that she was quite able to articulate the things she knew she must say.

"Mr. Carter — Edwin — please do not chide or blame yourself for our current situation. When you left I knew that things could not be certain between us. There were too many possibilities created by both time and distance. I did wait two years after receiving one very welcomed letter from you, which I answered, but receiving no further reply I assumed you had moved on and that you were lost to me. It was then that I mustered the courage to live a life that might not include you, and I sought opportunities which would give me security and an occupation to fill my days. I refused to become a martyr to misery simply because I had been abandoned, possibly through no fault of yours. For all I knew you had met with grave misfortune and were in serious difficulty, or perhaps dead. I also knew that you may have met someone and married. Many people go through such losses and they either ruin their lives with self-pity, or they find a way to contribute. I was attempting to do the latter."

He had leaned back in his chair and was listening intently, but he was alert to the dangers in what she was about to say. He wanted to know all about her, but he was not of a mind to hear of her falling in love with someone else and marrying. He started to speak, but she stopped him by holding up her hand. If she allowed him to interrupt here she might not have the courage to continue, particularly since what she needed to say was no doubt going to bring her to mortification.

"As you know, I had experience in millinery and had often spoken to you of having my own shop. I now do, and as it turns out, the business has fared very well. Bringing Martha in has only increased our popularity." Here was the difficult part to tell, but she must go on. He had a right to know.

"Before opening the shop, I was well-employed, and my life was quite satisfactory in every way, save one, so I set out to fill that particular void. What I did not realize was that the void was not male company in general — it was you." Mr. Carter near jumped out of his chair for joy, before recalling that she was someone else's wife. Mrs. Pearce did not notice his reaction and she continued, unaware.

"However, because I did not recognize the truth of that vacuum, I made myself available for matrimony. Several of my acquaintances had gentlemen friends they wished me to meet, and I did so, albeit without any real enthusiasm. There were dinners, the theatre and carriage rides, but no one satisfied. One was fat. One was bald. One had no sense of humor and others were either sadly ignorant or acutely rigid. I'm sure that makes me sound proud and condescending, but I am attempting to be absolutely honest here." She looked down at her hands and the gold band on her ring finger before saying, "In verity, although I did not admit the truth to myself at the time, the difficulty was that no one measured up to you." He quickly staunched the smile that threatened to break across his face as he realized she had evidently not yet met Mr. Pearce at the time she was describing. The "ideal" Mr. Pearce, who evidently possessed every virtue she required. She continued.

"You are no doubt wondering how I ever managed to settle on a husband, with my many requirements and a disposition that was so fastidious, but the truth is . . ." *Oh, how difficult this is, but I must press on.* "The truth is, I never did find him." Mr. Carter sat bolt upright and blinked several times. Surely, she was not about to say she had married someone she did not love, but somehow, by the grace of God, he refrained from interrupting. She must proceed at her own pace, relating things in her own way, but how he wished she would get on with it!

Mrs. Pearce closed her eyes and took a deep breath that seemed to last five minutes. Finally, she nodded and said, "That's right. I never did find someone I could love and be with for the rest of my life because I had already found him, but you were somewhere in another world. So, I settled for the spinster's life rather than commit to an unfulfilling marriage. I did, however, steadfastly refuse to be labeled a spinster since fashionable ladies often do not want to purchase clothing from a woman who could not attract a husband, and I was determined to finally become a shopkeeper." He definitely recalled her determination. It was one of the things about her character that attracted him at the time, but where on earth was this conversation headed, and when did Mr. Pearce appear on the scene?

"By then, my family was gone, and I returned to Bristol, to care for a great aunt who was in ill health. I remained with her for more than a year, until she died. Since I was heir to her small fortune it seemed a perfect opportunity, upon my return to London, to become the recently widowed Mrs. Pearce, who was opening a millinery shop. So, you see, Edwin, I became Mrs. Pearce in fabrication because in truth I would always be yours." *There! She had summed up her dismal and false existence in a few statements, and now he knew full well what a flimsy character she possessed. She had misrepresented herself to many people, including friends who trusted her. She was a fraud — a liar. No better than a criminal. It no doubt confirmed to him that he should be thankful they had not married.*

A naturally exuberant man, Mr. Carter had held his peace with difficulty while he listened to what he expected would be the summing-up of what he had lost forever, but with her last statement everything was turned topsy-turvy. He could contain himself no longer. He leapt from his chair, let out what sounded very much like an American Indian war whoop, grabbed her hands and pulled her up to swing her around in unexpected joy. Everyone had turned in their direction, their expressions disapproving, but he didn't mind. He didn't mind a bit, and he continued his celebration by shouting, "There is no Mr. Pearce! Ha! Ha-ha! There *is* no Mr. Pearce!!" Suddenly he stopped. Still holding both her hands in his, he set his face very close to hers and added, in a more private and commanding tone, "There never was a Mr. Pearce, and — hear me well, my girl — there never will be." Both of them began to laugh, relieved of the regret and heartache that had been compounded through the years. Eventually, Lucy managed to calm him enough that they could return to their seats, this time to order more tea and discuss the future, rather than the past.

Mr. Carter was all elation as he sipped his tea and gleefully thought to himself, *Poor Mr. Pearce, whoever he might have been, for he missed out on the best woman in the world!*

CHAPTER NINETEEN

Marley

Marley seemed a bit reticent. He was only in Scrooge's bedchamber because Scrooge had raised such a fuss and demanded that he make an appearance. Otherwise, he would not have floated over this threshold for at least another fortnight, or perhaps longer. Still, when one's "presence" was required, one must respond, even if the demand was made in a rather rude manner.

"Scroooooooge," he began, but his greeting did not elicit the usual reaction from Scrooge.

"Marley," responded Scrooge, "you are no longer required to make ghostly sounds and float about in order to convince me of your state of being. I am well aware that you now exist in the nether areas, dropping in when you are inclined to utter a few bits of wisdom and then simply disappear." His scorn was not lost on Marley even though, in the absence of mortality, Marley could no longer be truly offended.

"If my ethereal ears are hearing you correctly, old partner, you are feeling a bit out of sorts and I am chosen to take the brunt of your anger. Is that not so? Or am I misreading your temper?"

Scrooge sighed. "It is not anger, my friend, and I do apologize for taking my misery out on you." He sank into a nearby chair and shook his head. "Marley, I have many questions for you. I also have a few things to tell you, and I may even ask for advice, which I know you are always pleased to impart."

Marley laughed, and it was the first time Scrooge had heard him do so since his death eight years previous. No, in point of fact, Scrooge could not recall ever having heard Marley laugh, other than when that drunken cabby fell off his perch into a barrel, head first. At the time, Scrooge had simply grunted with disdain, but Marley thoroughly enjoyed the man's discomfort. Their behavior that day was testament to how much they had both changed, since then.

Just then, Marley looked directly at Scrooge and said, "I heard what you thought," and it was Scrooge's turn to laugh.

"Marley, as I said, there are several things we need to discuss, the first being a bit of information for you. Your old friend Edwin Carter has returned from America, where he made his fortune. He credits you for having loaned him the money and says you were told by a spirit – right here in this room, I assume – to give him the money."

"That is quite true, replied Marley, although I could not have called Carter 'friend' at the time. He was more a thorn in my side and living evidence that I had truly encountered a celestial being the previous night, which did not at all appeal to me. As you may recall, I spurned even the merest suggestion of the supernatural, and was convinced that we were born, we lived, and we died, and that was all there was to it."

"We both believed that, for the most part," interjected Scrooge. "The only thing that was 'real' to us was the feel of a pound note, or a sovereign, in our palms. How I wish I had not fallen for that mistaken idea of success, and wasted so many years!" He crossed his legs as if he were conversing with a live friend, and continued. "Isn't it intriguing, given our unbelief in the hereafter, that we would spend so much time accumulating money. What good did we think wealth would do us if we couldn't take it with us, and the very counting of it would amount to nothing, after our deaths? Why did we not at least spend it selfishly on ourselves, since we believed the years between birth and death were all there was to life?"

"Obviously we were not thinking. We were truly misers. Miserable, short-sighted misers", replied Marley, and Scrooge nodded in agreement.

"With regard to Carter," continued Marley, "I believe that may have been the one act of kindness, probably the only one I ever did in my life, that may have helped save me from the flames of Hell. Because of it, I began to see the truth of things. However, I am also aware that I made the loan out of fear, rather than heartfelt compassion. I am convinced that good deeds alone don't garner mercy because they can be done for selfish reasons, such as fear, or power, rather than love. I would go so far as to insist that redemption is a matter of belief, rather than works. However, if you believe what is right, you will act out that belief and do good, as a result."

Scrooge understood. He then uncrossed his legs and leaned forward in his chair, his elbows on his knees, before changing the subject. "Marley, I have several questions for you, but I will begin with the one that has rankled the most. Will you please tell me why you have consistently spoken to me in half-thoughts and riddles? Are you aware of how many times I nearly missed the mark, simply because I could not discern your meaning?"

Now it was Marley's turn to nod, and he replied, "I say what I am supposed to say," which gave no answer, whatsoever. Scrooge was annoyed, and wryly suggested, "Were the riddles and hints, then, designed to stir my brain and make me a better man, bit by bit, in the figuring?"

"Precisely," replied Marley, without adding anything more.

Scrooge was again irked, but he knew from previous experience with his dispassionate associate that he would get no more on the subject. For that reason, he asked a different question.

"Not long ago you slipped into my bedchamber and said, in essence, that I must choose between faith and fear. Then two others made the same statement. Although I believe I know the difference between faith and fear, and the possible consequences each choice brings, I am curious as to why you said such a thing, and why then."

"In case you have not taken notice, my friend," replied Marley, "I sometimes have pre-knowledge of dangerous or perplexing situations you are about to face. Or, you may have already begun to face them, but you do not know what to do. That is all I was imparting to you. I knew you were moving into a headwind, facing predicaments that could prove to be too much for you if you did not employ faith. You needed to keep moving, and it was a reminder that there was a way to do so."

Scrooge had more on his mind, but was hesitant to give voice to his thoughts since the whole idea was painful in the extreme. The truth was, he feared he had made a serious mistake that had resulted in a landslide of unnecessary agony and activity for the family and friends of Fred Symons. He had not spoken of it to anyone, since it could serve no purpose at this point, other than to expose his guilt and the suffering they might have escaped had Scrooge been more vigilant. Scrooge decided he could speak of it to Marley, however, and cautiously began his admission.

"Marley, there is something else. Not two nights ago, at 3:00 AM of the clock, I awoke in a sweat. I bolted straight-up in bed, a new and terrible idea filling me with guilt and remorse over what I feared had been a terrible oversight on my part." Marley nodded, and Scrooge continued, gradually allowing himself to speak of it without holding back for fear of censure.

"I did not allow Catherine to view Fred's body. I was certain it was for her welfare that I insisted she not look on his deteriorating flesh, but what if I had allowed her to do so? She was the one person in the world who knew Fred Symons on an intimate level. She knew every mark on his hands; the distance between his brow and his nose, and the very shape of his earlobes. She would have known these things, and she would have noticed the difference between Hugh's body and that of her beloved. Perhaps she would have taken one look and announced, "That is not my husband!", and the story would have taken a completely different turn. We would have avoided so much misery."

Marley was paying attention, although he did not seem surprised, nor put off by the information. He simply asked, "And what if she had done so? Describe to me the "turn" the story would have taken."

"Well,", began Scrooge, "for one thing, we would have known Fred was not dead. That, my dear departed friend, would have been momentous. It would have saved us all from a great deal of sorrow."

"And what makes you think you would have believed her?", asked Marley.

"Eh?", responded Scrooge, not expecting the question. "Why would we not believe her?"

"Well," said Marley, "There were three of you who would swear that the body was that of Fred Symons. Each one of you was convinced that Fred was dead, and you did not have a wife's sentiments to make you doubt that it was he who lay in the barge." Scrooge was frowning, trying to stay with Marley's line of reasoning.

With patience, Marley added, "Catherine, on the other hand, had a woman's need for her husband to be alive. Would you all have thought she was simply convincing herself that the body was not Fred's? Would you have been willing to allow the police to dispose of the body as an unknown, based on Catherine's statements, when all of you believed it to be Fred? I put it to you that, if that were the case, you might have questioned her state of mind, and you would have been reluctant to release the body to an undesirable means of disposal. No doubt you would have feared that she was fooling herself, and that she was going to live the rest of her life waiting for the sound of footsteps that would never arrive."

These were weighty thoughts, for which Scrooge had no replies, but he did see what Marley was suggesting. It was true that, had Catherine insisted that the body was not that of her husband, the mourning and the funeral might have been avoided, but Scrooge, Norris and Homer would have agonized over the possibility that the body truly was that of Fred Symons, and the end result would still have been the same. Fred had eventually re-appeared, and life had gone on. Either way, it would have been a very difficult situation, prior to his return.

Once again, as if Marley had heard what Scrooge was thinking, he remarked, "Let's flip the coin and move on to assert that there may have been some good come out of the 'death' of Fred Symons. Had you simply released the unidentified body to the police, based on Catherine's word, you would never have known of the existence of Hugh Weld, and he would not have been buried as one of the family. That may not be of import to you or many others, but I suspect it means a great deal to Fred.

"You also formed a closer tie with Catherine; and you learned how well-liked and respected is your nephew, and that is a thing worth knowing." Scrooge nodded and was a bit relieved of his guilt by Marley's insights. He would, nevertheless, continue to ruminate on the idea until he had truly settled it in his own mind. Unbeknownst to him, it would not take long to do so.

Merely four items had been ticked from Scrooge's list and he was prepared to spend the entire night in discussion, if need be, but just as he opened his mouth to move on the next question, he noticed Marley begin to fade. *Why, the unreliable . . .*

Scrooge stood and roared, "No! Don't you dare, Marley! You cannot leave now, just as we are finally carrying on a cogent conversation." His threat did no good however, because Marley had already faded to half his appearance as he uttered a diminishing "An-o-ther . . . time," and disappeared altogether.

"Marley!", barked Scrooge, unintentionally kicking the leg of his bed. "Ow!" Hopping around on one foot, he wished he could lay hold of one of those clanking chains and tie the spirit down! *Drat the obstinate specter! Drat him!*

CHAPTER TWENTY

A Mother's Sentiments

O n the day following their return from the villages Scrooge and Fred met with Rollo Norris. He was anxious to know if they were able to identify the dead man and was relieved to learn that they had done so. His name was Hugh Weld, and Scrooge and Fred had entered a certain pub by chance, and happened to meet the very men who knew Weld and had witnessed his death.

Weld lived with his mother outside the village near the locks, and neither of them was well-liked by their neighbors. In fact, Hugh had been loathed by everyone with whom they had spoken. The behavior of the townspeople toward Fred, when they believed him to be Hugh, was further proof of their disdain for the man. He evidently had no relations, other than his mother.

As to the death itself, Scrooge attempted to summarize for Norris. "It seems he was in the habit of picking fights and abusing others whenever possible, and one night he entered the pub where the same several men seem to congregate on a regular basis. He was clearly enraged over something and wanted to take it out on someone. No one paid him any notice except an older man who made the mistake of simply looking at him. That was all Weld required, and he threw the fellow across the room, then took hold of the man's cane and began to beat him with it.

"This was evidently the proverbial 'last straw' for the rest of the men, and the heftiest one in the room grabbed Weld, struck him, and says he was prepared to kill him. The others admitted that they were ready to join him in the effort when, of a sudden, Weld stood stock still, stared off into space and keeled over — thoroughly dead.

"The entire roomful of men witnessed it and verified that no one had killed him. They all agreed that he had definitely departed this world in what appeared to have been a very surprised state, with no one's hands upon him. However, because they feared they could be blamed, they devised a plan to rid themselves of the body without announcing that he had even died. People did find out of course, but no one cared, and in the meantime the men arranged to slip him onto a barge headed our way. And that, my friend, is how we ended up with the corpse. It was exactly what they had intended — that someone else would dispose of the body."

Norris pondered aloud, "I wonder why they resorted to such intrigue, rather than simply tell the truth and be done with it. As a constable I can tell you there were certainly witnesses enough to verify their story. Yet, instead, they devised a clandestine plan to dispose of the body, then carried it out. It would be an act that would hang over them for the rest of their lives, had you not wandered into the pub that day." Looking at both Scrooge and Fred, Norris added, "You understand what I mean. I refer to the constant fear of their subterfuge being 'found out;' the discovery of which would indeed cast suspicion their way. They acted as if they had, in fact, killed him."

"I have been considering that," said Fred, "and I believe they behaved as they did because they felt guilty, even though they were not culpable before the law. You see, all of those men had murder in their hearts. They wanted him dead and had wished it for years. Simon admitted he was ready to 'finish him off,' and the rest of them were ready to join in, though it turned out no one in that room actually committed murder or, I presume, even manslaughter."

Both Scrooge and Norris were looking at Fred with comprehension, and they agreed when he added, "Had they not harbored such animosity toward the man it would have been much simpler for them. They would have reported the incident, explained that he died of natural causes, and each would have supported the others' statements. As it was, I believe their guilt caused them to panic, which drove them to treat the death as if it had been murder because, in their hearts, it was. They feared being accused of killing him simply because they wanted to. The idea was already living within each of them, and they all knew how close they had come to actually committing the act."

"And the mother?", asked Norris. "Did you speak with her?"

"We did not," said Scrooge, "although I believe we should. I feel a responsibility toward her, not only to inform her of what happened, since evidently no one has taken the time nor made the effort to do so, but at least to give her the benefit of knowing why her son seems to have disappeared, and to tell her that he has been buried in London. The poor woman must be beside herself," looking at Fred, "as we were when we thought we had lost you, my boy."

It was agreed that Norris need not accompany Scrooge and Fred. The dead man's identity had been discovered and it was not a case of murder, so, Norris' investigation would be closed. The rest was a matter of whatever Scrooge believed was the right thing to do. Scrooge would, of course, offer to move the body to the woman's choice of burial place, since he felt it was the least he could do, considering the grief this was going to cause her.

೮ვ৪০

Following their meeting with Norris, it was another three weeks before Scrooge and Fred could make the trip to speak with Mrs. Weld. As luck would have it, Homer had engaged the very same driver, who was waiting with his carriage as Scrooge and Fred disembarked from the train. The poor man's surprise at seeing Fred was pronounced. He knew it was the same unfortunate he had driven not one month earlier, but the transformation was unbelievable. Whatever the wealthier man had done, his magic had worked. The poor blighter was a different man! Had the driver not seen with his own eyes what Fred truly was before, he would not have believed such a change was possible, right down to the way he spoke his words. It was an outright miracle, that's what it was!

Scrooge gave the driver Mrs. Weld's direction without noticing the driver's dubious expression. Thinking he must have heard wrongly, the driver asked, "You want to go there? Are you certain you want to see that woman – Mrs. Weld?" Curious, Fred responded, "It is. Why do you ask?"

"Well, o' course it's none o' my concern, is it, but it's just that she don't receive visitors – ever. She's prickly, she is, an' she don't seem to have the sensibilities of a regular person. It's no easy task to try to carry on a decent conversation with her. She don't talk back 'n forth, like. She just yells 'n carries on, an' it's got worse over the years. When she first come here she weren't so bad. Oh, she were never pleasant, but she weren't so much a harpy as she is these days." It wasn't exactly a warning, but Scrooge and Fred both prepared themselves for what could prove to be a difficult undertaking, although Scrooge was convinced that the news of her son would be welcomed, even if heartbreaking.

In less than an hour they found themselves outside a derelict cottage. It appeared to be abandoned, other than an emaciated dog who barked at their arrival before disappearing behind the house. Fred noticed the poor dog's tail was wagging, and he wanted to jump from the carriage and give him some pats on the head, but the animal was making himself scarce. Scrooge asked the driver to wait or return within the hour since he did not know how long the interview would take. He knew how grief could extend things, as it often demanded the time to give comfort and reassurance. Poor woman.

It took three times rapping on the door before they heard someone shuffling about inside. When the door slowly creaked open they were unable to hide their surprise. Scrooge would later recall that the woman who answered the door put him in mind of the wicked witch in *Hansel and Gretel,* who took children captive. At the time he reckoned that sorrow could do that to a woman, particularly if she did not know what had happened to a missing child.

"What do you want?", she snarled. Her English was better than Scrooge would have expected. At least it was better than her son's, or Fred's successful imitation of him. "I don't take to visitors, so you'd best be off, the both of you." She was closing the door when Scrooge said, "We are here to speak to you about your son, Hugh. We have news of him that we are sorry to have to impart."

There. He had prepared her for the worst and hopefully made a way for them to enter, which proved to be the case. She slowly opened the door, still considering whether to bother with them, or not. Finally, she allowed them in and Scrooge's earlier thoughts of Hansel and Gretel turned to how they would have felt once they were actually trapped within the confines of the witch's home. Mrs. Weld's worn-out cottage was dark and unfriendly, much like her countenance, and it conjured the sense of being snared by the witch who would gladly roast them in the oven, if only she could.

The three of them continued standing until Fred suggested, "Perhaps we should all sit down," and she begrudgingly indicated two rickety chairs, which they gingerly took. Mrs. Weld sat in a worn overstuffed chair near a fireplace that hadn't hosted anything warm for some time.

As they sat, the woman looked at them closely for the first time. The dimness of the room precluded detailed examination, but it was obvious she believed she was face to face with her son — the one she evidently did not know had died. Scrooge was immediately concerned with the terrible blunder they had made, barging in on this woman without warning, presenting themselves to her in this manner and completely forgetting the resemblance between Fred and her son. This poor, poor woman. How she would feel when she realized, as quickly she must, that this was not her son and that he had, in fact, died. Both men were searching for the right words to assist her through this heartbreaking revelation when she stood and pointed at Fred.

"You! What are you doing here? I told you to take that mutt and leave, and I meant it. I never wanted to see your face again, so you can just take your new suit and your fancy friend here and march right back out the door to wherever it is you came from!" Suddenly suspicious, she squinted and asked both of them, "Why are you here? What is it you want? I've got nothing for you!"

It was beyond belief! Where was the concern, the motherly love, the worry over a son gone missing? Scrooge must at least let her know this was not her son. "Mrs. Weld, this is not Hugh. I am Scrooge and he is my nephew, Fred. I realize he greatly resembles your son, and I apologize for the shock this brings you, but we are here with news of him. Are you up to hearing it?"

"I am not a missus!" Nor am I a maiden, but I never married." As she spoke, Mrs. Weld appeared confused and slowly wagged her head, eyeing Fred with a sidelong stare, examining him. "I can see, now that you say so . . . he is not Hugh, although I would have thought . . ."

Scrooge continued using the title "Mrs.", since he did not know what else to call her. He shifted in his chair and softened his tone. "Mrs. Weld, I do not know quite how to tell you this, but your son did not leave, exactly. I am very sorry to say that he died in the village, apparently of natural causes, and his body has, through circuitous circumstances, been buried in London." He may have imagined it, but for an instant he saw in her expression a stab of pain over the son lost and gone forever. Then, as quickly as it had shown itself it was forcibly rejected, to be replaced by her usual dour countenance. So, he continued, not knowing what else to do. "I can understand how upsetting it must be to have a loved one disappear following a serious quarrel . . ." and was immediately interrupted.

"Loved one? You think I loved him?" Her cackle was brittle and ugly, and not entirely believable. "I didn't love him. I refused to love him because he cost me everything I ever wanted. I had earned the right to detest him from the time I knew he was a part of my body, and he continued to be a heavy weight I carried for all of his life. But for him I would have had a high situation. I would have been a lady! I wished he had never been born, and I told him so!" She eyed Scrooge suspiciously and asked, "He's dead, you say? Truly dead and gone from my life — finally?" Again, that fleeting expression of loss, quickly replaced by long-practiced animosity and self-pity.

Although he could scarcely believe what he was hearing, she seemed willing to talk, and Scrooge persisted with the first thing that came to mind.

"Then you weren't worried when he simply disappeared? You told him to leave and you assumed he had done just that?" *The men at the pub said he was more out of sorts than usual – angrier – and seemed to be looking for an excuse to act on it.*

"Yes, and I was glad of it. I was finally rid of my feckless spawn, and his presence would no longer remind me, day after day, of what he had cost me." To further document her grievances, she added, "He left that dog, Milo, behind - to trouble me, no doubt. I will not be troubled, however. Since I have no way of putting the animal down, I have stopped feeding it and it will either run off, or die. Either way, I will at last be finished with both of them!" Scrooge and Fred suspected they were hearing a scripted speech, but it had been rehearsed and nurtured for so long that it had become her true character. It had smothered any maternal sensibilities she may have otherwise allowed herself to possess, much less exhibit.

Could this get any worse? Fred had to ask, "How did the birth of Hugh keep you from achieving your plans for success?" He had an inkling, but wanted to hear the story from her, if for no reason other than he was beginning to feel sorry for Hugh. It was becoming evident why the man had been so angry and hateful.

Mrs. Weld sat a little straighter, as if admiring her youthful self in a mirror. "I was pretty. Very pretty, and I had a way about me that men liked. Though you may think otherwise from what I've said, I behaved myself until I went to work in a fashionable house." She was finally willing to divulge secrets and they were certainly not going to curtail her. "I was a parlor maid, so of course I was occasionally noticed by the family, even though we were warned by the housekeeper to stay out of sight. I did so at first, but then I began to make certain that the master, who was a widower, got a glance of me now and then. It worked, because he found in me something he liked. Naturally, one thing led to another.

"He said he would marry me. He said I could be important and would be the lady of the house, and I believed him." Her expression turned bitter when she said, "It would have happened too, I'm certain, had I not become with child. When I told him, I meant for us to marry quickly, but he denied everything because it was inconvenient for him at the time, and he would not be budged. He insisted some other man was responsible and said I should apologize to the other servants for bringing such shame to them. He accused me of all sorts of things that were untrue, and tossed me from the house without reference, and without pay."

"What did you do? Where did you go?", asked Fred.

"I had a distant cousin who lived right here in this cottage, and I had just enough money to make the trip. She took me in and kept me, as well as the coming child who had cost me everything. When she died fifteen years ago, we stayed on. She owned the cottage and left pittance enough to keep us alive — as paupers. Hugh earned a few shillings here and there, but he always wasted it at the pub."

It seemed there was little else to say, other than to offer to move Hugh's body. Scrooge no longer believed the idea would be welcomed, but he made the suggestion nevertheless. She declined ungraciously, asking why she should want his remains to be laid nearby. He was fine right where he was, and she would be glad to never hear of him again. Nor did she inquire as to how, or why, he was buried in London, much less how he died. She refused to care. It was a decision she had made concerning Hugh years ago, and it was too much a part of her thinking to allow for any grief now.

They stood to leave, but out of politeness Scrooge allowed that if she should change her mind she could contact them in London at the counting-house of Scrooge, indicating himself, and Symons, motioning to Fred.

Mrs. Weld stood stiffly at attention. "Symons!" she abruptly cried. "Your surname is Symons?" She stepped toward him menacingly and snarled, "Who is your father?" This conversation had suddenly taken a turn no one could have predicted. With some hesitation he could not explain, Fred guardedly replied, "My father was Geoffrey Symons," which caused Mrs. Weld to back up unsteadily and collapse into her chair. Eventually she was able to ask, "You are *his* son? And your mother died shortly after you were born, in 1819?" Fred nodded. It was too much, but she suddenly understood. It was clear to her what they were about. "I was told you died in childhood, but you are not only alive, you and your fine friend have come to taunt me, have you not? How dare you come here to exhibit how much you have in the way of worldly goods, and how much I lost because of my son — your worthless brother!"

Brother! Fred stiffened. Had they heard her correctly? He struggled to take it in, but his ears were roaring, and he could barely absorb this news. His brother? Half-brother to be exact, but near twin in appearance.

"I assure you, ma'am, we had no idea of yours or your son's history until this very moment." It was Scrooge who somehow managed to make the statement, since Fred was immobile and finding it difficult to react in any manner.

They need not have concerned themselves with how to leave gracefully after receiving such astonishing news, because they were immediately set upon with a broom and chased outside to the sounds of a great deal of shouting. The indignations and injustices Mrs. Weld had self-righteously embraced for so many years had finally found two objects on which she could pour it all out, and she was not going to forego the opportunity.

Their driver had an inkling of how things might end and was waiting in the lane, not far away. As they ran toward the carriage Fred yelled, "Good man! Let's move quickly!", and both he and Scrooge clambered aboard. Upon hearing Fred's voice, Milo darted from his hiding place and leapt into the carriage too, jumbling things a bit. Fred grabbed him and held on tight as the driver shouted the horse into action, and they were off at a gallop.

CHAPTER TWENTY-ONE

What's to be Done with Hugh

A fter fleeing from Mrs. Weld, Scrooge and Fred returned to the Tring railway station, but not before stopping at the butcher for a few pieces of meat, which Milo downed in quick gulps. Fred was adamant that the dog should accompany him in the first-class rail car, but a railway agent insisted the dog was not "up to snuff." Fred was in short temper and not of a mind to heed an arbitrary directive, so the agent eventually threw his hands in the air and allowed what he considered a prodigious break with railway etiquette. Once ensconced inside the car, Milo sat on the floor beside Fred's feet and it was not long before he lay down, gave a loud yawn and placed his head on Fred's foot. He did not sleep, however, but kept his eyes open for any unknown danger.

Both men were very quiet on the trip back to Town, other than to agree in abject disbelief that there could be a woman, or a person of either gender, come to that, who could be so cruel and hard of heart. It was astonishing that she was able to place so much blame on those around her, even on a son who did not ask to be born, and attribute absolutely no wrong-doing to herself.

Fred was lost in thoughts he could not contain, nor control. All of these years he had had a brother of whose existence he knew nothing, who had suffered terribly at the hands of his nefarious mother. Fred's mother had been virtuous and kind, but she had died not too many weeks after he took his first breath. His father succumbed three years later, and Fred's Uncle Scrooge placed him into the care of a very kindly couple, Mr. and Mrs. Barnes, who loved him dearly. They had been wonderful guardians, but both were gone now. He had also had the privilege of attending good schools, and never wanted for anything. He had been given so much, while his brother had nothing. He wanted to mourn for the man his brother had been, and even more for the man he might have been.

As the rhythm of the railroad noises signified their movement toward London and all that it represented, Fred realized one of the worst things about this discovery was the fact that he had actually pretended to be his brother, to a much too realistic extent, and in public. It was as if the brother with everything had ridiculed the brother with nothing, and it made him heartsick. Had he known, he would have been unable to go through with it. If only Uncle Scrooge had been made aware of Hugh's existence early on. Things would have been much different, indeed. Perhaps the two brothers could even have grown up together, but it was too late for such imaginings. With that sad truth settled, Fred leaned down and lovingly stroked Milo, his brother's one – and only – treasure.

There was much to discuss, but neither Scrooge nor Fred was up to it at the moment. During one of their minimal exchanges however, they did set a time to meet for tea at Fred and Catherine's the following afternoon. They could discuss the entire episode in detail then, since each would have mulled things over during the night. Fred specifically requested that Scrooge bring Mrs. Langstone, to contribute her astute thinking to the discourse.

As Fred continued to ruminate on the past several weeks, a thought occurred to him which he spoke aloud. "Uncle, do you suppose I will ever be free of my father's totally dishonorable legacy?" Scrooge could only shake his head and say that he sincerely hoped so, for surely this must be the last of Geoffrey Symons' misconduct that could ever touch him.

ϘϚ

Teague, the Symons' Spaniel, was less than overjoyed at the sight of Milo. However, Lily, the housemaid, thought him the sweetest animal she had ever seen. He was medium in size, with black and white hair, some of which was long enough to be rather matted. His ribs were close to his skin, but she could change that, given the chance. Fred gave the dog over to her care, to see what she could do to improve him and make him comfortable.

Milo was first given a good meal, then a warm bath, which included Lily as he shook off enough water to give her a thorough showering.

Next (and with permission to be away from her duties), she combed him for near an hour, carefully snipping those bits of matting that refused to yield to the comb. Finally, a dry Milo was furnished with a blanket over a soft pillow that was laid on the floor in a warm spot in the kitchen. Milo had never been spoilt and thought himself the luckiest dog in the world. He made a nest in his bed by walking on it a few circles first one way, then the other, and plopped down for a well-earned, safe nap. His appearance truly had been improved, and the end result was quite an attractive border collie mix. It wouldn't take long for Lily to put some flesh on those bones of his, and then he would be a very handsome boy, for certain.

 C3&O

The following afternoon Scrooge and Mrs. Langstone met Fred and Catherine for tea at the Symons home. Catherine had heard a few details of the trip to the villages, but Mrs. Langstone had heard nothing, and both were anxious to learn more about the dead man's family. Scrooge began as soon as the tea had been poured and the delicious fare offered around.

"My dears, I must say this has been an extraordinary three months. Each of us here has had adventures beyond our imaginations, yet we still have a bit of unfinished work. Before we arrive at that topic, however, perhaps we should recite the most recent occurrences, to ensure that all of the pieces have fallen into place. That will also bring the ladies up to the present. What say you, Nephew?"

Fred agreed without hesitation, but he put it to Scrooge to recall the most recent events.

"I am certain we do not need to enumerate every detail of the spring, since we well remember those terrible events. Fred, on the night of your return from the 'dead' you were given the particulars of what took place whilst you were away."

"And what a welcome I had!", laughed Fred. "I could not for the life of me understand what the commotion was about." The irony of his choice of words did not escape him, but he let it go by. "All I knew was that my expectations of a return to a quiet house, to slip noiselessly into my bed and get some well-earned rest, were the opposite of what I encountered. It was a mad house! People were running about in their nightclothes, screaming and batting me about the head and shoulders, and Teague was carrying on as if he were the town crier!" Everyone laughed, recalling how the fear and despair over Fred's "death" had suddenly been turned into joy, even though it took a great deal of commotion to get there.

Continuing, Fred recounted his walks in the villages and his very limited experience as a "ne'er do well." He tried to relate his sentiments by saying, "It was frightening how easily I slid into 'being' that person, whoever he was, and came to behave as he may have done. In my heart I had begun to feel shamed, downtrodden, and even violent, particularly when those boys pelted me with rotten produce!" Catherine had already heard some of this story, but Mrs. Langstone was visibly stunned. He paused momentarily, then said, "But the worst, I believe, was the pain of learning that this poor lost and hated soul was, in fact, my own brother."

"Brother!", cried Mrs. Langstone. She was not expecting such news and was openly astonished. "He was your brother? Truly?"

"Yes," replied Scrooge, "which accounts for his uncanny resemblance to Fred."

"But . . . how? How could he be Fred's brother? And if he was, why did neither of you know of his existence prior to now? Oh, this is beyond anything!" Mrs. Langstone was clearly perplexed, but anxious to understand.

"He was despised," said Fred, "and that, inconceivably, included being detested by his own mother, a contemptible Mrs. Weld. She hated him with a passion that began before his birth and she reminded him of that fact daily, for his entire lifetime. It was no wonder he became an outcast. He had nothing other than his dog Milo, who is now happily installed in our kitchen!"

Mrs. Langstone was shaking her head. "But why . . . how . . . could a mother reject and hate her own child? Something must have been terribly, sadly wrong within her." Returning to the fact that they were brothers, she asked, "Then, Geoffrey Symons was his father, as well as yours?" She shook her head. "Oh, my. May I ask for more information? I don't want to pry where I shouldn't, although I am curious as to whether this involved Fan, and which of you sons was the elder."

"It's quite alright," answered Scrooge, who recollected that Mrs. Langstone knew Geoffrey since she had been a particular friend of

Fred's mother, Fan. Scrooge explained, "Hugh's mother became a maid in the Symons home sometime after Fan's death, although I don't know how long after, so Fred is the elder. Hugh's mother believed Geoffrey was going to marry her, but when he found she was with child he turned her out, and he died within a year, or so. She was left with a baby she did not want, and rather than attribute the blame where it rightfully belonged – to herself and Geoffrey – she blamed Hugh for ruining her chances of becoming the lady of the house, and she never forgave him."

Obviously feeling sympathy for Hugh, Fred said, "So he became what he was, and she never changed her opinion of him, nor does she see that she, herself, may have done anything amiss."

Mrs. Langstone sat back in her chair, dazed. Who would have imagined such goings on, although she must admit that she was not surprised at Geoffrey's behavior since she had, long ago, become aware of the defects in his character. She was, after all, close to Fan and spent a great deal of time in the Symons home when they both were young. In fact, she was with Fan at Fred's birth, and was holding Fan's hand when she died.

It was Catherine's turn to ask, "And what about the mother? She is not really 'family' since she and Fred's father did not marry, but Hugh certainly was related. And what about the grave? I understood from you, Fred, that she does not want his body moved, to be laid near her. So, I am wondering, why not leave him where he is? We would, of course, need to re-think the headstone, but that is a simple business, is it not?"

Everyone agreed with the idea, but then the issue of what to inscribe on the headstone arose, and they soon realized that the wording might not be such a simple matter, after all.

"We couldn't very well say 'beloved,' since we didn't know him, and what little we do know suggests he was anything but 'loved' by those who were acquainted with him", said Scrooge.

"He was my brother, nevertheless," interjected Fred, the stating of which led him to express another thought. "We were half-brothers, and extreme in our differences, but I can honestly say I feel I know him, somewhat. That is a result of having 'walked in his shoes' for only two days, but it was enough to form some opinions, particularly after meeting his mother, and to feel true empathy for him." As Fred was speaking he did not notice that his wife, uncle, and Mrs. Langstone wore expressions of unexpected understanding, as well as respect.

Continuing that line of thought regarding Hugh's gravestone, Fred said, "Perhaps we could come up with a few words that do apply. I can name two or three. 'Brother,' and the date of death, although we do not know his birth date, nor the exact date of his death, and we certainly will not revisit the mother and The Bald Parrot, to inquire. Possibly the word 'unfortunate' could be used?" Seeing their reactions, he said, "No? Well, we could also add the word 'son.' Both 'brother' and 'son' are true, although they meant little, in his case."

"Perhaps a Scripture verse would apply," suggested Mrs. Langstone. Catherine nodded her agreement, and proposed, "Something along the lines of, 'The Lord is merciful,' or a similar statement of grace that would apply in this case. Perhaps we could ask Rector Gifford?"

"From what you ladies have just suggested, an idea comes to mind," said Scrooge. "Why not simply inscribe his name, 'Hugh Weld,' then the dates of his life, in years. We know he died in 1845 and we can guess he was born in 1821. Then a Scripture verse, such as one I recall from the Second book of Timothy which says, in part, 'The Lord grant him mercy in that Day . . .' It is certainly something we would all hope for the poor man."

The other three were in agreement, and it was decided. Scrooge offered to take care of changing the headstone, then ventured to mention one more thing.

"Because of the connection to you, Fred, I believe we should make some sort of settlement on Mrs. Weld, hateful as she may be. I expect that she will accept it without giving thanks and will most likely believe it should have been more. What say all of you?" He was planning to do it, no matter what they said, but was interested in their reactions. It took a moment before they answered, and even then, they were hesitant. It was Fred who spoke.

"Uncle, I won't argue if you feel you should, but I must say she has done nothing to deserve it. In fact, her abominable behavior would suggest she has earned nothing other than the life she is now living," and the women nodded slightly. They did not want to appear hard-hearted, yet they definitely agreed with Fred's sentiments.

"I understand," replied Scrooge, "and I won't make it an enormous sum, but I believe Fan would wish it." That was all it took, and everyone immediately agreed. So, Scrooge made up his mind as to an amount and arranged through Homer to have the monies delivered to Mrs. Weld. Naturally, Scrooge did not receive a response.

C3&20

There was still the matter of Milo. What an attractive, happy and well-behaved dog he was, and Fred was very fond of him. Teague, however, was not like-minded, and Fred was unsure of how to proceed. Since Fred enjoyed Milo, he let the dog accompany him to the counting-house one day. It happened to be a time when Peter Cratchit was in the office to assist in small ways, which included delivering papers.

Fred and Milo were immediately greeted with, "Ah, this must be Milo," and "Here, boy! That's a good fellow!" He was given many pats and rubs behind his ears before he lay down, out of the way, between Homer's station and an interior wall. When Peter asked to take him on a delivery, Fred saw no reason not to allow it, and they bounded from the building as if they were best mates. When they returned an hour later, Peter was ebullient. "He is such a good dog, so well-behaved, and so friendly," he cried. He had not stopped petting him since their return, while Milo leaned comfortably against his leg. After glancing at his father, Peter looked at Fred and ventured to ask, "Are you seeking a home for him then?", and everyone knew what would follow.

"We have a yard now, and children to play with," said Peter, looking directly at his father, his eyes full of earnest appeal. Cratchit was not giving any indication of acceptance or rejection of the boy's plan, and in the ensuing silence Peter presented his best argument. "He could run with Tim and help him to grow even stronger!"

Fred and Cratchit looked at each other while Peter ventured to utter one last word. "Please?"

Cratchit gave a small nod to Fred and they both laughed, which allowed Peter to immediately flop on the floor alongside Milo and hug the wonderful dog that was now his — his, and all of his siblings', of course. So, it was settled. Milo would have a wonderful home; Teague's world would return to normal, and Fred could see Milo whenever he wished.

CHAPTER TWENTY-TWO

The Cratchits

The Cratchits had resided in Camden Town most of their married life. Their six children were born there, and they were attached to their community, even though it was certainly not the grandest in London. Eighteen months ago, when Scrooge had raised his salary, Cratchit suggested to his good wife that they find a better, or at least a larger, living situation, but she was not enthusiastic. She had countered with, "We are happy here, are we not, and some day it will be just the two of us again, and then we would be in a house that was far too large." It was true that they were happy but, as the husband and provider, Cratchit deeply wanted to improve their lot, and was determined to do so. His wife's argument against his wanting to improve things, "whether or not it makes us happy," caused him to halt his plans for well over a year – until he stumbled onto the perfect site in August of 1845.

"My Dear," he announced, "I have found a home with enough space for all of us and I don't want to hear your argument that it will be far too large when the children are grown and gone. That is the very time we will need more space, with the many grandchildren I expect to have! It is not far from here, so we will not have to begin all over in a new neighborhood. It has the amenities I so want for you, and it is quite the thing!"

Mrs. Cratchit agreed to view the potential home and was so pleased with the house and its situation that she insisted they move as soon as possible. Within the space of a month they had emptied their old house of their things and were happily ensconced in very comfortable rooms. Together they blessed Mr. Scrooge for making it possible.

When Cratchit announced the move at the counting house, Scrooge immediately determined to visit the new home and bring a gift. Cratchit was vastly valuable to him and Scrooge thought so much of him and his entire family that he honored them at every opportunity. Today he would bring them a fine English china tea set, with plenty of cups and saucers. He knew Mrs. Cratchit would like them and he was certain they would be used. She was not one to put things away so that they remained new, while she grew old.

"Why it's our Mr. Scrooge," cried Mrs. Cratchit warmly as she answered his knock. He was holding a parcel, and two others sat next to him on the step. "Bless me, what's this?", she asked, giving every indication of being very pleased. He said, "You have a new home, and this is a gift to bring additional cheer to an already happy household. I have something for the children too, but I would prefer to leave the

218

largest parcel out of sight – perhaps in another room, for the time-being?"

They both entered the home and he carried her parcel while she led the way with great anticipation. Mrs. Cratchit showed him where to set it down, then she and Scrooge retrieved the other packages from the stoop. With some hefting he deposited the larger package out of sight in the dining area while she placed the smaller in the parlor. Mrs. Cratchit quickly unwrapped her tea set and clapped her hands together as she exclaimed, "Oh, my! How very pretty this is! So lovely. Thank you, Mr. Scrooge. Thank you very much. That is kind of you. We will certainly enjoy using these!"

Suddenly realizing that this was his first visit since they moved, she cried, "You have not seen our new home! You must allow me to show you 'round before I give you a nice cup of tea!" Obviously pleased, she pointed toward the back and explained, "Mr. Cratchit is so enjoying having a garden that he spends much of his time there, although he does share it with the children and Milo, of course. I'll tell him you're here." With that, she stuck her head out the door, called "Coo-ee!", then said, "He'll be in directly, and you take note, Mr. Scrooge, of what I wager will be a smile on his face. Yes, that garden is his delight."

Scrooge couldn't be happier for them and, surely enough, Cratchit's smile was wide when he greeted Scrooge. He was that pleased to be his employer's friend as well as his employee, and found it difficult these days to recall just how grueling Mr. Scrooge had been, two years previous. Cratchit could still recall his astonishment when Mr. Scrooge turned into a totally different man, overnight.

On Christmas Eve 1843, Scrooge had snarled at Cratchit and made it clear that he very much resented the fact that he must let him off work the whole of Christmas Day, never mind that the entire city of London would be celebrating. Cratchit toiled in cold and discomfort under the auspices of a stingy slave-driver all the other days of winter, so he had chanced to say that yes, he would like the entire day off, and had begrudgingly received it. He knew the workday following Christmas would bring worse treatment from Mr. Scrooge, but it would be worth it.

That had not been the case, however. When Cratchit was a bit late arriving at the counting-house on the day after Christmas, Scrooge growled and led him to believe it would be a very difficult morning, indeed. It still gave Cratchit goosebumps to recall his employer's surprising words. Instead of the usual threats, he had raised Cratchit's salary to a very fine living. It also quickly became their practice to keep a good fire going, and Cratchit found he could now easily move his fingers in the comfortable warmth of the office. It was beyond belief, yet it was true. They later discovered that Mr. Scrooge had also anonymously sent the Cratchits that prize turkey on Christmas Day. It not only fed the entire brood, but provided extra meat for his good wife to prepare further meals!

Since that time Mr. Scrooge had adopted the family, given Cratchit another increase in salary, and made certain their needs were always met. One of those needs had been Tiny Tim's health. Because of Mr. Scrooge's generosity, Tim now had the best physicians in London, as well as the best of care, and was thriving beyond anyone's dreams. In fact, the family continued to call him Tiny Tim even though it no longer applied, as he seemed to be growing taller every day!

As if on cue, the children realized Scrooge was visiting and ran in to greet him. Martha was at the millinery with Mrs. Pearce, but the others gathered close and near leapt on him, crying, "Uncle Scrooge! Uncle Scrooge!" Tim and Milo were playing outside with the neighbor boys, but soon came running in. Milo flopped on the floor and Tim placed himself on Scrooge's lap, then leaned on his shoulder. Scrooge nearly wept as he saw the boy actually running, and the boy's affection was worth more than all the pounds silver that Scrooge had ever earned.

"Now, my dear family," announced Scrooge, "I have something for you all." With that, he pointed to the package wrapped in brown paper. The children were polite and wanted to make certain, so they asked, nearly in unison, "Is it for us?" Scrooge nodded in the affirmative, which brought on more questions. "May we open it? Now? Is it for something special?"

"It is for you in your new home and yes, you must open it forthwith. I insist upon it!" With that, they tore off the wrapping without harming the contents, and when the gift was revealed the children were speechless. They stared. They held their breath. They looked at Scrooge and asked once again, "Are these truly for us? Are they ours – to keep?" He nodded, and they exclaimed, "Puppets! Punch and Judy puppets! Oh! Thank you, Uncle Scrooge! Thank you!!" As each child took a puppet and began to experiment with its handling, Belinda excitedly cried, "Perhaps we can build a theatre, with a curtain and everything, and we can put on a show for each other, and even for the neighbors!"

"As to that," said Scrooge, "there is a puppet theatre in the other room. Please fetch it and begin practicing for your show immediately!" The children screamed and ran, totally absorbed by the excitement of their new venture, lost in the joy that a simple toy can generate in a child's heart.

Mr. and Mrs. Cratchit thanked Scrooge for his generosity and kindness, and he reassured them by admitting, "You know, since Christmas close to two years ago now, I have learned that it is truly better to give than to receive." Knowing that he was sharing more than was required, yet trusting these decent people with a few of his innermost thoughts, Scrooge said, "I can assure you that I gain a great deal from the joy your children feel when I present them with something I believe they will use, and it far surpasses the small amount I give in its purchase."

Anticipating their fears, he promised, "I will not spoil them, but, on occasion, if I know of something that will give them pleasure and help them in some way, with your permission I will give it to them as long as it is not outlandish. I pray you will tell me if I ever overstep in my giving." The Cratchits knew he meant what he said, and they were appreciative, not only of his provisions, but of the fact that he was mindful not to overindulge his "nieces and nephews."

It had not escaped Scrooge's notice that the Cratchit children were well-behaved and mannerly. To a person they were unselfish, creative and achieving in their studies. They were special, every one of them.

No, they were not perfect, but they were delightful. The miracle of it was that their parents had managed to produce such people and they had done it with very little income, thanks to the former miserly Scrooge. It was a lesson to him that money was not the answer. Character, discipline, and sacrifice made the difference. If only he had known that truth while he was still in his youth, and even into adulthood.

Out of curiosity, several months earlier Scrooge had asked each child what he or she would like to do when fully grown. Their answers were as unique as their personalities. Martha, of course, had chosen her path and was becoming an excellent milliner under the tutorship of Mrs. Pearce. She was, nonetheless, expecting to marry someday and would strive to be as good a wife and mother as hers had been. Peter, even though he occasionally helped out at the counting-house, had a real talent to build things. He read and observed all he could about engineering and was certain this current age of industry was going to fulfill his every desire. Why, he might even become famous!

Belinda wanted only to marry and be a mother. She had decided against six children, however, and preferred to have three, who would be well supported by her very successful husband. The younger girl and boy were too little to have serious intentions, so the girl's heart was set on becoming a gypsy, and the boy insisted that he was going to be a street lamplighter. Tim, possibly because of his earlier illness, had definitely settled on becoming a physician, perhaps even an excellent surgeon. He, as well as his siblings, believed it was important to help others wherever possible. They had been taught, and learned well, that one's happiness usually came best by contributing to the happiness of others.

No matter how well their children were turning out, Mr. and Mrs. Cratchit had their worries, and right now they were most concerned about dear Martha, who was receiving attentions from two men. They would never have told her they were concerned, for fear she would misunderstand and conclude that they did not have confidence in her. They did, however, occasionally discuss their uneasiness with Mr. Scrooge. Today the topic was raised again, once the children had disappeared to play with their puppets.

Over a very good tea and cake, Mr. Cratchit said to Scrooge, "I don't say Martha doesn't have good sense, because she does, but sometimes youngsters can be pulled in the wrong direction without knowing it." His frown deepened as he added, "I suppose part of the difficulty is that none of us knows what direction would be the right one, so we cannot even advise her."

In response, Scrooge applied logic and commented, "Yet, if you are concerned about her choosing rightly between Homer and Rollo Norris, are you not suggesting that one of them might be wrong? Is that your fear?"

It was Mrs. Cratchit who replied. "I don't know that either of them would be 'wrong' for her, but I suspect that one would be 'better' than the other. The men are very different, and their lives will become even more dissimilar as they age. I simply want her to be in the best possible situation, to increase the likelihood of her happiness. But then, I suppose it is also possible she will not marry either one, and will marry someone with whom she is not yet acquainted, so perhaps we needn't spend much time thinking on this."

"I realize I should not ask this," interjected Scrooge, "but since it is at the center of your concerns, can you say which man you would prefer, based on the knowledge you have of each one?" He could see that the question made them both uncomfortable because they did not want to voice such a thing, for two reasons. In the first place, it was the sort of thing one could not "undo," and once said, it would remain said forever. If she married the one they had not preferred, anyone who had heard them voice a preference for the other would always know. In the second place, they realized their preference might not be the best man for their daughter.

Scrooge immediately regretted the question and begged that they not reply. He did not need to know. In fact, if asked, he would refuse to voice his preference for the same reasons. Scrooge could, and did, however, ask a different question. "Who does Martha prefer at this point? Has she said?"

It was Mrs. Cratchit who carried on most of these sorts of conversations with Martha, so she laughingly replied, "I believe her preference varies with the amount of time she has spent with one or the other. As you know, a courting man tries to make the best impression possible, and after she has conversed with one, she will sing his praises. 'Oh, Mother, doesn't Rollo say the cleverest things?', or, 'Oh, Mother, isn't Homer the most thoughtful man!', and on it goes. So, you see, it is difficult to know her mind, for it seems to change daily."

"Perhaps that is because she does not know it herself," interjected Mr. Cratchit, and they all agreed to drop the subject since they had reached an impasse. Instead, they finished their tea in conversation about their young Queen.

When it was time for Scrooge to depart, the entire family followed him to the door to say their good-byes. The children thanked him again, as did Mr. and Mrs. Cratchit, and he thanked them for their hospitality. What he really wanted to say was, *I thank you all for enriching my life. You have no idea how much it means to me to be considered part of this family. To think, had it not been for those persistent spirits on Christmas Eve 1843, I would still be a lonely, mean old man – to myself, and to all of you!*

Instead of going into all of that, however, he simply received their affection and exchanged it for his.

CHAPTER TWENTY-THREE

New Life

Mrs. Langstone and Catherine spent many hours together during the summer months as Catherine prepared for impending motherhood. Having an older, experienced and caring friend had been a God-send for Catherine, and she revelled in the opportunities to learn from Mrs. Langstone, as well as lean on her for support. The strong connection they formed was as devoted and tender as mother and daughter, which filled a void for both of them, and it would remain for the rest of their lives.

Flora was always welcome during their conversations and she visited often, but, as the younger sister, Flora was even less knowledgeable than Catherine in matters of marriage and motherhood. She did, nevertheless, pay attention when Mrs. Langstone gave advice because . . . well . . . one never knew when one might marry and find one's self in the same situation, did one?

Over tea, and sometimes as they simply sat together outside, the women discussed life, husbands, motherhood, and disappointments. It was during these conversations that both Catherine and Flora discovered what a wise and learned woman was their friend, Mrs. Langstone. She was also kind and very patient when dealing with youthful ignorance.

During one particular tête-à-tête between Catherine and Mrs. Langstone, Flora stopped in for an unannounced visit. Because she thought so much of the older woman, she joined the two of them eagerly. Their conversations were always interesting to her since she was the more naïve of the two sisters. She was always welcome, and quickly made herself at home. "May I inquire as to what you are discussing?", she asked.

Catherine replied, "I was asking Mrs. Langstone how to stay attractive to a man. He may love and adore you when you marry, but isn't it likely that his adoration will fade once he has spent a great amount of time with you, and knows all of your little foibles? And how about the reverse? How do we wives remain attached to our husbands to the point that we still enjoy their society, and look forward to spending time with them?"

"Oh, I have wondered that myself," added Flora, who had not yet truly admired anyone, much less had a serious suitor. It was the sort of thing on which young girls spent much time ruminating, even before it became an actual fact in their lives.

Mrs. Langstone began speaking, and both women were rapt - anxious to hear whatever she might say. "When a woman agrees to marry," she began, "I believe several things should be considered before she enters into what will most likely be a life-long relationship. That is a long time to spend tied to someone who is not pleasing in his character.

"Not the least of these is the fact that she should respect him – think highly of him – and enjoy his company. That is generally only the case when the two agree on the important things in life, such as what they believe, what they like to do, and how they treat others." Here, she paused to add, "I suppose one could say that I am not 'up to date' with my advice however, since I have been a widow for several years." Because she was so comfortable in Mrs. Langstone's presence, Flora asked, "But do you not expect to marry again? I believe you should!"

Mrs. Langstone laughed, and replied, "I have not been seeking another marriage, but I suppose I would consider such a thing if I met a man who was a good match for me, and I for him."

The irrepressible Flora blurted, "Why, then, you must marry Fred's Uncle Scrooge! He is the perfect companion for you!", before she realized her remark was rude and that she had taken an inexcusable liberty. She immediately covered her mouth with her hand and said, "Oh, I do beg your pardon, Mrs. Langstone. I don't know what came over me, and I pray you will forgive my outburst."

Without addressing Flora's remarks regarding Uncle Scrooge, Mrs. Langstone simply smiled and said there was nothing to forgive because she knew there was no ill intent on Flora's part. The conversation then moved to Catherine's questions regarding the months before giving birth, the challenges of being a new mother, and her search for a nanny or, as some might still call such a person, a dry nurse.

Their time together and the topics they addressed were characteristic of many pleasant and informative afternoons Mrs. Langstone spent in the Symons home throughout the summer of 1845.

CB&CO

On a fine day in the fall, when the sun shone pleasantly as if to showcase the changing foliage and illuminate the country harvest, the men at Scrooge and Symons counting house were engrossed in their tasks. Without warning, a messenger burst through the door and announced, "Fred Symons! I'm lookin' for Fred Symons. Is he hereabouts?" Hearing his name being shouted, Fred quickly appeared in the front office to say, "I am Mr. Symons. What do you have for me?" He assumed it was an urgent dispatch on some matter of business.

"You're to go straight home – right now, if you please, Sir. I asked 'em to write it out for me, but they said you would know, and I was just to tell you you're wanted because your good wife is about to . . . well, they said she's gonna . . . she's . . . there's a babe comin'!" Everyone heard the message and ceased work immediately, with all eyes on Fred. Scrooge jumped up but Cratchit restrained him by saying there was a very important contract that absolutely must be prepared and signed that afternoon. So, it was quickly agreed that Scrooge would come to the Symons home after that particular piece of business was completed, which would be as rapidly as Scrooge could hurl the thing together!

Fred flew into motion. He quickly pressed some coins into the messenger's palm, and mistakenly pulled Homer's hat onto his own head — a bit askew, since it was a different size. He then had difficulty with his overcoat, having somehow managed to turn one sleeve inside out. Refusing to take the time to put it right, he left that half of the coat dangling from his shoulder, grabbed his walking stick and dashed outside. He left the door wide open, so everyone observed his running back and forth in the street, bellowing for a cab that seemed to take hours to appear. One finally did show itself and stopped to take him on. After losing his footing twice, Fred successfully leapt aboard, and they were off, leaving shouts of his direction echoing throughout the thoroughfare.

"Oh, my," remarked Cratchit when the ruckus had died down. "I say, this is exciting, and I'm not certain I will be able to concentrate fully until we know the outcome. It's a bit like Christmas, isn't it? We know there is a gift coming, but we don't know what it will be!"

Everyone enjoyed Cratchit's little joke, but no one was able to maintain a disciplined thought for long during the whole of the afternoon. Scrooge managed, with Homer's help, to complete the necessary papers for signing by an investor, and occasionally one of them managed to interrupt whatever the others were doing by remarking, "I wonder how things are going," turning all conversation to "Poor Catherine" and the very anxious Fred.

Cratchit put forth the wager that the baby would be a girl, since his good wife was absolutely insisting that it would be so. Homer, on the other hand, was expecting a boy, and Scrooge was of no opinion whatsoever. He had no preference, so long as it was a healthy child and would grow up thinking of him more as a grandfather than a great-uncle. He thought to himself, *I don't know why that should be important to me since I am not the child's grandfather, but perhaps that is exactly the reason. I am a blood uncle to Fred and the young Cratchits consider me an uncle, but I want a grandchild! I would, after all, be the only grandparent the child would have, so perhaps it is not such an outlandish wish, after all. Children need grandparents.* Yes. That explained it. The child needed a grandfather, and he was happy to oblige!

⚬₰⚬

Fred arrived home in a great deal of disarray. He had managed to right his overcoat, but forgot to pay the cabby, who chased him up the steps, loudly demanding his money while hammering on the door after it was slammed in his face. Having taken care of the oversight by vastly overpaying the man, Fred bounded up the stairs two and three steps at a time. He was stopped short of entering Catherine's bedroom by Flora, who shooed him back downstairs, to wait. Wait! How could he just sit there and do nothing when his dear wife was going through such a thing? What were they doing to her up there?

Mrs. Langstone was already with Catherine when the message was sent to Fred, and she continued to stay by her side. Out of pity, Dr. Kaye wandered down the stairs, where Fred stood pacing, and all Fred could do was look at the man wide-eyed and anxious. He wanted to grab the doctor, shake him until he blithered, and demand to know what was happening with Catherine. Since the doctor was an elder practitioner, he recognized the symptoms and held up both palms to Fred as he said, "Now, now, Mr. Symons, you needn't worry. At this point nothing much is going on, but I feel certain you will be a father by early morning, if not before." Then he turned to go, leaving Fred with very little in the way of information, which only increased his trepidation.

Just then Lily flew by, carrying towels or some such thing, and was gone so quickly he couldn't have grabbed hold of her apron strings to stop her, had it even occurred to him. Oh, this was too much! He needed answers. Finally, he retreated to his library where he found Teague standing at attention on a leather chair, staring at him as if awaiting marching orders. Together they sat, listening for any sound that might indicate something. Anything. Every minute seemed like an hour. Perhaps he should have remained at the counting-house, but he would have done no better there, and Uncle Scrooge would be here anon. That thought did not particularly encourage however, since Scrooge knew no more about these things than Fred.

Knowing how busy the maids were, rather than bother them, Fred wandered down to the kitchen, hoping to ask cook for a cup of tea. It was clear that the impending birth was on the minds of everyone when she placed a pot of hot water before Fred, having forgotten to place the tea inside! They both laughed a little at the oversight, and soon Fred was sitting at the servants' table, sipping as if in a trance.

Lily scampered down the stairs in a state. She was out of breath and did not realize the master of the house had invaded her territory as she exclaimed, between short gasps, "Oh . . . Mrs. Adley . . . it's terrible, it is! Poor Mrs. Symons is . . . sufferin' so. I don't rightly know . . . what to do, n' that's the truth . . . so I just do as I'm told . . . 'n right now . . . that's to get some hot water." She failed to notice Mrs. Adley's attempts to shush her by waving and pointing to Fred. When he sprang up in response to Lily's statements he nearly scared her out of her wits, and she jumped backward with a high-pitched squawk.

"Suffering, you say? What is going on, up there? Tell me! Is something amiss?", he cried.

Poor Lily had no idea whether anything was amiss or not, since she had never in her life observed or assisted in childbirth, so she could not come up with a reply. Instead, she simply stood before the master, flapping the air with her hands. Her behavior only contributed to Fred's upset, so he turned, dashed up the stairs and slammed headlong into Scrooge, who had just entered the house.

"Uncle!", blared Fred. "Catherine is suffering! We must discover what is going on up there! I've tried, but they won't let me near her!" He was near tears and since Scrooge was of an already unsettled mind, he was easily sucked into Fred's turmoil. He quickly turned to charge upstairs and demand some answers! Fred was following close behind, but they were thwarted at the landing by Mrs. Langstone, who accurately assessed their states of upset.

Forgetting their agreement to use their given names only in private, Scrooge nearly screamed, "Rebecca! Give us answers! How goes dear Catherine? Is anything amiss? What must we do?"

Mrs. Langstone placed her hand on Scrooge's arm and her palm firmly against Fred's breast as he attempted to push past her. "Now, you are both to listen to me. Catherine is doing all that is natural, and she is in no danger. If she were I would have come to you directly and advised you of the situation." Looking at them with an expression of motherly chastisement, yet understanding their agitation, Mrs. Langstone garnered their agreement to remain downstairs until she, or someone, gave them more facts. To herself, she thought, *waiting for a loved one to deliver a child is difficult for men who are accustomed to being in charge. Not only are they unfamiliar with the process, there is little to nothing they can do, and they are not used to that. Poor Ebenezer. Poor, poor Fred!*

As the afternoon wore on, nephew and devoted uncle mostly walked the floor of Fred's library. Teague walked with them until he finally gave up and stretched out on the rug for a much-needed nap. He could not sleep, however, for the feet tramping all around, and his eyes continued to keep a watch on his master. The men had been effectively shushed for the time-being, but were still anxious and were good for nothing other than worrying about Catherine. They did make several attempts to discuss business, but their efforts failed because, when one of them could concentrate, the other was unable to think of anything but what was occurring upstairs.

Eventually both men settled wearily into Fred's comfortable chairs, having resigned themselves to a state of ignorance, until they heard Catherine scream. It was somewhat faint, due to the distance between her bedroom and the library, but discernibly unlike the scream of fright that Fred heard the night he returned from the dead. No, this was undeniably a scream of pain. Horrible suffering. *Oh, Dear One!* Fred jumped up and ran to the library door, ready to wrench the thing open and fly to her, when Scrooge grabbed him from behind and wrestled him back to his chair.

"It will do no good for you to interfere, my boy. This is where we were told to wait, and wait we will." With that, they returned to a very unsettled silence. They were resentful, afraid and helpless, but silent. The few times they thought they heard a scream, they steeled themselves to the fact that they would do no good by interfering and their place was right where they were, like it, or not! In addition, Fred had begun to feel inexplicably guilty, which only added to his trepidation.

Lily brought the men some tea and sandwiches and they nibbled at what looked good enough, but felt and tasted like sawdust in their mouths. Who could eat with all of the horrid things happening to Catherine? In early evening Mrs. Langstone appeared at the library door to bring information. They nearly leapt on her, demanding details.

"Catherine is struggling a bit, and Dr. Kaye says it will help if he bleeds her, but she is adamant that he will not. He says she must either cooperate fully, or engage another physician. I have never seen the two of them at such odds, but there it is, and I will admit that I side with Catherine."

Before any more could be said, both men bolted from the library and bounded upstairs, bursting into Catherine's room without polite preamble. This time nothing and no one could have prevented them. Fred rushed to her side and was horrified by her state. As Flora wiped Catherine's brow with a cool cloth, Fred held her hand and pleaded with the Almighty to comfort and spare her. Dr. Kaye approached the bed, looked down his nose and announced, with a hint of disdain, "Your wife, Mr. Symons, is refusing to allow me to give her appropriate treatment. If she persists in this behavior I will be forced to withdraw from the case. I will not be responsible for her welfare, nor the baby's, if she does not submit to bloodletting."

Catherine looked at Fred with fear, and weakly begged, "Please, my love, do not allow him to take mine and our baby's life's blood. We both need it, I am certain. I feel it in my heart."

No more need be said. Fred turned to Dr. Kaye to say, very simply, "My wife will not submit to bloodletting, and there's an end on it." Scrooge then jumped into action and sent for his physician to come to the home forthwith. In a cool huff Dr. Kaye quietly put away his tools, closed his bag, nodded to everyone in the room and said, "I wash my hands of this delivery, both literally and figuratively. You are behaving recklessly, but I wish you well." With that, he left the room, walked slowly downstairs and out the front door. His injured pride had dictated that Catherine Symons was no longer his patient.

Scrooge's physician, Dr. Easton, arrived within the hour and assessed the situation. Then he spoke to Fred and Scrooge on the landing and said, very calmly, "We are doing alright, but I may have to give the baby a bit of assistance." The men were once again banished to Fred's library, but were less fearful than before Dr. Easton explained the situation to them. He had provided details of what he planned to do, promised them that he would not bleed Catherine, and assured them that he followed the new idea of washing his hands before and after childbirth. It was enough to allow them to return to a more normal state of mind, and they could now wait in hopeful expectation rather than abject fear.

Sometime before midnight Mrs. Langstone again knocked on the library door. Both men jumped up as she entered, and in their weariness, they nearly collapsed in relief when she happily announced to Fred, "You have a very beautiful son."

As the proud great-uncle pounded the new father on the back, Fred expelled a large breath he had been holding, and quickly followed the happy news by asking, "And Catherine?"

"She is fine, but quite exhausted. Everything went well, and she is resting. The doctor will return in the morning and says you may see her, but for only a moment. Mr. Scrooge, I'm sorry, but you must remain here. I'll stay with you." Fred flew from the room and Scrooge and Mrs. Langstone sat down, side-by-side. Sitting together, they rejoiced over the successful birth and the narrow escape from the well-meant, but questionable practices of Dr. Kaye.

As they waited in Fred's library, Scrooge remarked to Mrs. Langstone, "I hate to think of what may have happened to both Catherine and our dear little one had she not held the line with Dr. Kaye." It was true, and Mrs. Langstone nodded in agreement. Throughout the summer Mrs. Langstone had agreed with Catherine as she insisted that she would not be bled, and she had been pleased to see Catherine stay with her convictions. The whole bloodletting idea seemed rather barbaric to Mrs. Langstone. She viewed it as a practice that drained the very thing that the body required in order to remain alive. After all, wasn't it the bleeding that everyone attempted to staunch, following a serious injury? And if the bleeding could not be stopped, did not the victim perish?

Once inside Catherine's room, Fred crept to her side, took her hand and kissed it before kissing her forehead. She opened her eyes and whispered, "Have you seen our son?"

"Not yet," he admitted, but he stood as Flora brought a tiny bundle for him to hold. Fred had never felt so clumsy as he took his offspring and looked on him for the first time. The baby seemed a bit squashed and very wrinkly, but it made his heart race. His son! His, and Catherine's. Suddenly he was soaring. Never was there such a day. Never was there such a child. Never was there such a wife!

From that day on, the household fell into a routine that included a no-nonsense yet very loving nanny, and the sound of a wee baby crying at odd hours, but it was all delightful. Catherine was doing very well, and the baby was thriving. In fact, his son began to look like a real person to Fred. He noted that the baby was, indeed, extremely handsome. Fred had a great deal for which to be thankful and he admitted as much in his prayers each night, and every time his precious family came to mind.

CHAPTER TWENTY-FOUR

He Loves Me, He Loves Me Not

Edwin Carter and Lucy Pearce were more in love than ever, if that were possible. Their grief at the loss of each other had at one time settled into a dismal mass that hovered over each of them as they carried on with their separate lives. Although they had both been successful, the success had not satisfied, which gave all the more reason for these days to be filled with the wonder of renewed love. Mr. Carter was the more buoyant of the two, but both were absolutely overjoyed at this turn of events. He would have married Lucy the day he found her again, but they finally agreed to marry without wasting a great deal of more time, and settled on the month of December in order to begin the New Year as man and wife.

There was one possible problem, and Mrs. Pearce was apprehensive as to how to approach the matter. It was generally assumed that a married woman's time would be solely employed in the care of her household and family, but she had developed a successful millinery and was not anxious to absent herself from its operation. Oh, she could sell it and make a good profit, which would possibly keep Martha and Rose employed, but she had no wish to do so. In fact, she very much desired to remain the proprietress for as long as it satisfied. The problem was that she was uncertain as to how Mr. Carter would react to such a suggestion. Edwin was fairly traditional in his views regarding the relationships between men and women, as was she in the main, but she did not wish to give up her business. Finally, over tea one Sunday, she broached the subject.

"Edwin, my dear, there is something on my mind and I need to discuss it with you, but I pray you will listen without prejudgment and will wait until I have fully explained myself before responding." She knew him to be a fair and kind man, so she asked, "Will you do that?"

Surely, he would, and he could not imagine that she would have anything on her mind with which he could not totally agree. The two of them were so alike, so of one mind, so in love, that nothing could come between them. "You tell me what it is, my dear, and I will wait until you have finished before I make a reply."

"Thank you, Edwin. I knew you would do so." She dabbed the corners of her mouth with her napkin and began. "As you have seen, I have a very pretty little business on the Strand. I am not only proud of it and have supported myself well from the profits, I find that I very much enjoy my work." He was nodding in agreement at all she said. *Such a wonderful woman. So industrious, and I am prodigiously proud of her.* He could foresee a successful marriage in their future — a marriage others would surely envy.

Mrs. Pearce continued. "You are the most important person in the world to me, and I am very anxious to begin our life together, much as we had planned many years ago, but one thing has changed, and I do not desire to change it back." *What? What could she possibly want to retain? No matter. It must be a small thing and nothing of note.*

"Edwin, please understand, Dear. I do not plan to sell the shop." He was not upset, and she was relieved. In fact, he replied by saying, "I see no reason to sell the shop, since it is very successful and is a testament to your abilities when you were on your own. No, I see no need to sell."

"Oh, Edwin! I knew you would understand, and I'm so pleased. Not only will I be married to the best man there is, I will be able to carry on with the activities that I love. Of course, it will not take time from us, since you will be busy throughout the days, and if we need a holiday, Martha is quite capable of managing for a time."

Edwin sat back, his expression one of utter amazement. "What? I have no objection to our retaining ownership of the millinery, but do you mean to say that you want to continue to be a shopkeeper after you become my wife?" He could not believe his ears! "Do you fear that I cannot support us? Is that what is behind this thinking? If so, I can assure you I have enough wealth to carry us into our old age, were I not to engage in business another day!" By now he was working himself into an upset and was questioning her faith in him.

Oh, dear. It is, after all, as I feared. "Now, Edwin. I said nothing about your ability to provide for me. I am only trying to tell you that I plan to continue doing what I love."

"So, you will not love being my wife? Will that not be enough for you? How have you come to this conclusion without ever having been my wife?" Now the exchange was beginning to resemble an argument, rather than a discussion.

"And how can you assume that I would be happy letting go of an occupation I enjoy, simply because I have married? I am not a young lass, you realize, and I have tasted success in commerce." Both were feeling ill-used, and if it continued, the exchange would likely not end well. But since good sense does not always reign during vexation, the confrontation intensified.

"Mrs. Pearce," he purposefully used her pseudonym, knowing it would hurt her and create distance between them, "I see no reason for you to doubt my place as the head of the house, and it is my intention to live with a wife, not a shopkeeper. If you cannot, or will not, enter into a marriage contract on that basis, then I am uncertain about our marrying, at all!" He had said it, and the moment the words rolled over his tongue, he knew he had gone too far. There was no way on this earth he wanted to lose her again, but he had his pride, and he would not grovel. No, sir!

She was close to tears and feeling quite misunderstood, but she would not be bullied into living a life that consisted of all things wonderful except for the one thing she desired in terms of occupying a goodly portion of her time. She had a talent and she enjoyed the service she gave. She did not see how that could take away from a husband, particularly if he were to follow his own heart's desire in terms of how he spent the majority of his time.

Neither spoke. Nor did either appear to be reconsidering his or her stand. Mrs. Pearce took a sip of tea, and he stood. "Come, Lucy, and I will walk you home. I believe each of us has a great deal to ponder, and at this moment I seriously fear it will not end as we had originally planned." She was heartbroken, but independent enough, after the past years of supporting herself, to refrain from saying anything that might indicate she would give up her livelihood, or that she was of a mind to end the engagement. She realized he was upset and not thinking clearly, and she would give him room to expend his vexation. He, on the other hand, simply wanted to be away from this woman who was not at all who and what he had believed her to be!

C3&O

Lucy spoke to Martha about her plans to continue the shop after she married but did not mention that it had caused a rift between her and Mr. Carter, so Martha did not consider the news confidential. Without intent to gossip, she mentioned Mrs. Pearce's plans to her parents, thinking it would settle their minds with regard to Martha's retaining her employment. Naturally, they made interpretations and formed some opinions regarding the news. When they were finally alone they followed through with their own discussion.

Mrs. Cratchit began the conversation. "I cannot see why Mrs. Pearce would want to continue managing the shop once she has her own home and a husband. It will certainly be enough to keep her busy, I would think. But then, perhaps Mr. Carter is of a mind to think it is a good thing. Perhaps he is pleased to have her doing something of her own."

Mr. Cratchit parried with, "I have spoken with him and I will simply say that he is not pleased with her intentions, and I suspect they are not conversing – on this topic, or any other. I am uncertain, however, if it is the fact that she wishes to keep the shop, or her need to do so, that most worries him. And too, my dear, you must remember that you not only had a home with no servants, which I am certain she will have, but you also eventually had six children to care for. That would be enough to keep any woman busy and, hopefully, satisfied. They are also marrying later in life, and she has lived as a single and very independent woman for quite a few years. It might be a bit frightening for her to think of making such momentous changes all at once. She may view leaving her business as a fearful loss, rather than a gain."

It was odd that Mr. Cratchit was inclined to see Mrs. Pearce's viewpoint, whereas his good wife believed Mr. Carter was "in the right, on this one." She did ask Mr. Cratchit, however, "What did you say to the man when he told you of Mrs. Pearce's intentions?" Smiling a bit, he replied, "I said the love and devotion of a good woman was a rare and a precious gift, and that no matter how 'perfect' the woman is, there will be disagreements and two viewpoints on many things. I asked him if he were willing to sacrifice all that they had for a disagreement that could certainly be solved through rational compromise."

"And what did he say?", asked his good wife.

"Nothing. He did not answer, but I know he heard me and I believe he is, even now, considering what I said. At least I pray so."

Mrs. Cratchit was pensive. "I do hope the idea of maintaining the millinery shop will not come between them to the extent that they cannot get by it." Looking at the ceiling while tapping her cheek with her finger, she said, "I wonder . . . perhaps we should invite them both to an evening of games with the children." Mr. Cratchit understood immediately and agreed that it should be done forthwith. They would each be sent an invitation and would not be told that the other was also invited. It was somewhat dishonest, but would be done with the best of intentions!

‹З&О›

Mr. Carter and Lucy Pearce had not seen each other for several days, and no letters were exchanged that contained either pleas, or censure. It was a difficult time and neither wanted to entirely give in nor, with painful finality, put an end to a relationship that had taken so long to come to fruition. Both of them were in agony during those days of being absent from each other, and each was praying that the other would come to his or her senses. When they received invitations to an evening of games with the Cratchits, each accepted, unaware that the other would be there. Neither was in the mood for frivolity, but the Cratchits were wonderful company and could only lighten their current humor.

Mr. Cratchit felt somewhat guilty about the subterfuge but reasoned away his guilt by talking to himself. *Something needs to be done, my man, so it might as well be done by you. Those two love each other and there is a way, I'm certain, to work it out, but first, we must get them to talking again. If it doesn't succeed as planned, we won't be the worse for meddling unless Mr. Carter no longer desires my society, but it must be chanced.*

Mr. Carter was the first to arrive at the Cratchits' and was enjoying their company very much. He was entertaining the family while delivering his hearty laughs when there was a knock on the door. Mrs. Cratchit answered, and Lucy Pearce entered. She did not see Mr. Carter immediately, but he spotted her. Instead of the pique he had coddled for over a week now, he felt nothing but happiness and a need to take her in his arms and reassure her that all would be well . . . until she smiled back at him. At that moment he recalled the insults she had inflicted on his manly character. She would not get away with it and simply win him over with a smile, not on her life! He would be polite from a distance, but that was the absolute limit.

When Mrs. Pearce saw his smile fade, she knew they were back to where they had left things several days earlier, and she reacted in kind. No smile. No pleasant words. Perhaps no talking to each other at all. If that was what he wanted, then that was what he would have, shame on the man! Perhaps she would be well rid of him, after all.

The Cratchits carried on as if nothing were amiss. Tiny Tim suggested they play, "I Am Thinking of Something," and the other five children loudly agreed. The Cratchits had their own rules for the game and insisted that the person who was "It" could only name something that was in the room and within plain sight of everyone.

Peter Cratchit said he would be "It" for the first round, and after everyone gathered near (with Mr. Carter and Mrs. Pearce deftly avoiding each other by remaining as far apart possible) he announced, "I am thinking of something small!"

"Is it alive?", asked Tim, not realizing that the only "live" objects in the room were the people therein. There were no plants, and Milo was outside, patrolling his yard. Besides, it was something small.

"No."

"Is it pretty?", asked Martha.

"Yes."

"Is it painted?" Mr. Cratchit must ask something, after all, and that was the only question he could think of.

"No."

"Is it shiny?", asked Belinda. She liked pretty, shiny things.

"No."

"Is it worn by a person?" Belinda, again. She would be adorned with beautiful things someday, she was certain.

"Yes."

No one appeared to notice that Mrs. Pearce and Mr. Carter were involved in their own game of not joining in the merriment. Neither was putting any sort of effort into making guesses as to what Peter was thinking. Instead, they sat at opposite ends of the group, refused to look at each other and attempted to appear normal by donning unhappy smiles. The Cratchits managed to carry on the game, in spite of them.

"Is it mounted on metal?", asked Tiny Tim. If it was worn, it must be attached somehow, although he was unsure of precisely how that fit his question, other than a metal pin, perhaps.

"Yes."

Mrs. Cratchit asked, "Is it carved?" She had an inkling, and asked the question to verify her suspicion.

"Yes."

With that, Martha cried, "A piece of jewelry!"

"Yes, but that is not the answer."

Then, Mrs. Cratchit won the round by quickly adding, "You are thinking of the lovely cameo Mrs. Pearce is wearing, are you not?"

"Yes, I am!", declared Peter, and the entire group loudly applauded how quickly the puzzle had been solved, and how astute was Mrs. Cratchit.

What the Cratchit family did not know was that the cameo was recently given to Mrs. Pearce by Mr. Carter. He had made the purchase in New York and brought it back hoping she would receive it as a love gift. The fact that it had been the object of this game resulted in serious discomfort for Mrs. Pearce, considering the current state of her relationship with him, but it gave pause to Mr. Carter in a much different way.

Mr. Carter's mind was reeling. He could feel, even now, how his heart had longed for her when he made the purchase, and how he thought he would burst with happiness and pride as he saw her finally wearing it. His sensibilities for the past nine years had undergone so much turmoil, beginning with the high hopes for the two of them as he left England. How lonely he had been in the ensuing years, dreaming of her and planning their future. Upon his return he had faced the worst possible disappointment as he learned she was no longer his. Then, miracle of miracles, his sorrow had been turned to joy as he discovered that she was his, after all, and always had been. She had remained faithful to him.

Within the span of a few ticks of the mantel clock Mr. Carter's thoughts raced through the last decade and their recent reunion, and his resentment dissolved. His stubbornness was useless and would only serve to do them both harm. No, he had too much regard for this extraordinary woman and he would not toss it away in a temper. Blast it all, he had believed her lost to him once and would not go through that again — not for all the submissive housewives in the Empire! She was worth everything to him and, if he truly loved her, he should want her to be happy. They were no longer children, after all, so they both had their talents and their accomplishments. They could find a way to be contented, and to be satisfied with each other in the doing of it. He was not about to push her away from him now — not after all they had each been through, to come this far!

Without ceremony and before a large audience of captivated Cratchits, Mr. Carter rose from his chair and quickly crossed the room to Mrs. Pearce. In doing so he publicly and irrevocably sealed his choice. It was a decision he would never change, and never regret.

CB&O

The following day Edwin Carter and Lucy Pearce resolved the problem of the millinery. They agreed that it would be inappropriate for the shop to take precedence over her time with her husband, but they were also aware that Mr. Carter would be away from home most of the day, and occasionally for several days, depending upon his business enterprises. Mrs. Pearce had been alone for many years and being alone, per se, did not upset her, but she did need to fill the time with the things she knew and enjoyed. She assured her future husband that she would definitely manage their home and would not let the millinery interfere with those duties. In fact, she was looking forward to caring for him and their household, but did not want to be limited solely to domestic endeavors.

It was decided that, during the hours, or days, Mr. Carter was away on business, Lucy would see to the shop. That would, of course, be most of the time, at least most of the daylight hours, but if there were occasions when Mr. Carter was "at home," Lucy would also be home, and Martha would manage the shop. Lucy trusted her implicitly and it would be good training for her. If Martha had a problem she could send a missive via messenger to Lucy, who would reply as to how to handle it. Both Mr. Carter and Lucy Pearce expected that she would, at some time in the future, turn the shop fully over to Martha, to manage. She might even sell it to her, but for the time-being Lucy required the constancy of what was familiar to her.

 Cʒℰꝅ

Mr. Edwin Carter and Miss Lucy Edgar were married December 6, 1845 in the Church of St. Michael, with Rector Colin Gifford officiating. The couple had purchased a comfortable home in Belgravia and it was there that the wedding breakfast was held following the ceremony. Guests numbered less than thirty, the list being limited by the fact that the groom had been away for many years and neither the bride nor the groom had family still living. Mr. Cratchit acted as best man to a very nervous, yet ecstatic groom, and Martha Cratchit served as Maid of Honor. Everyone agreed it was an extremely uplifting and heartwarming service, and that the bride was as lovely and happy as any they had ever seen.

CHAPTER TWENTY-FIVE

Christmas Day

It was finally the Yuletide. There was no snow to speak of, but London was cold, creating scattered patches of ice that young boys used for sliding, and Scrooge thought it all absolutely delightful. It was a time he now thoroughly enjoyed — the holly, the carols, the giving of gifts and the "good will toward men." Fred and Catherine were hosting Christmas Day this year and their guests had gaily gathered in their home. They included Mrs. Langstone and her mother, Mrs. Sotherton; Rector Colin Gifford, Constable Rollo Norris, the new Mr. and Mrs. Carter, Dick and Priscilla Wilkins, and Flora. Homer Probert was invited but had graciously declined as he had previously accepted an invitation to spend the day with the Cratchits.

Scrooge was in deep thought as he sat in a very comfortable chair in the parlor, near a beautiful Christmas tree. Catherine had insisted on having one since hearing gossip that the royal residence had at least one decorated tree, and she was quickly learning how to out-do the Castle. The tree candle lights and the warmth of the fire created a peaceful mood and Scrooge let his mind wander. As had become his habit, when he let go the reins of his mind it invariably wandered to thoughts of Mrs. Langstone — even on Christmas, in someone else's home, and in the midst of a good amount of activity. He couldn't help it.

It was now slightly over a year since Scrooge and Mrs. Langstone were introduced at a gathering in November 1844. Since Mrs. Langstone had been Scrooge's sister Fan's friend, they had actually met many years earlier, but Scrooge did not recall the occasion. Mrs. Langstone remembered him however, and after conversing for some time they found themselves dancing the waltz with a great deal of ease and style, and their friendship developed from then on.

The two of them agreed on most things that mattered, such as faith, family, politics and a generality of interests. Those topics on which they disagreed were either unimportant, or easily ignored. Both were readers and they enjoyed plays, musicales, and outings. They were conversationalists and appreciated excellent dining. Much of their time was spent in each other's company, with an ease that usually came from friendships that had existed for much longer. Yes, they had had their difficulties, but for the past few months Scrooge's biggest concern seemed to be the matter of what to do, if anything, about their regard for each other. At least, he prayed the regard he held for her was mutual.

Any declaration of love would be required firstly of him, not her, and since he had not managed to do so, he felt like a complete and dismal failure. He was pitiable — no better than a shy, tongue-tied schoolboy when it came to words of love. He simply had not been able to say them. The truth was, he did not know exactly what to say, or when to say it, in addition to not having the smallest notion of how to go about it. Following his conversation with Priscilla Wilkins, Scrooge had become more convinced that what he felt for Mrs. Langstone was truly love, but the knowing had not made it any easier for him to do something about it. In some ways it made it more difficult because the stakes were now higher, but he was unsure of the odds.

Perhaps he was spending too much time pondering the entire thing, but he was helpless in the face of love. He would have been mortified had anyone been aware that he had even stood in front of his looking glass, practicing how to declare himself. He would sometimes imagine Mrs. Langstone seated beside him, or facing him, while he invented and rehearsed various approaches, quickly casting each idea aside as silly and ineffectual.

My dear Mrs. Langstone, you cannot be unaware of my sentiments where you are concerned. Such humbug. It was too formal and having to make a response would place her in an awkward position.

Rebecca, my dear, for some months I have known . . . Worse yet. If he had known it for some months, why was he just now saying it?

I must ask you, Rebecca. Have you any feelings for me? Definitely not! She would think him a cad for asking her to declare herself first, and she would be correct!

Marley had said to simply take things on faith. Priscilla had agreed, and even his rector had confirmed the idea. Scrooge did not, however, believe that taking a leap of faith meant putting on a blindfold and jumping from the nearest cliff! So, he had continued to do nothing and had not committed to any sort of action where Mrs. Langstone was concerned, but time was not standing still.

With a bit of effort Scrooge managed to put all thoughts of undeclared love aside and determined to enjoy the company of his friends and family on this wondrous Christmas Day. He rose, stretched a bit, and joined the others. Catherine had gone upstairs to speak with the nanny, but everyone else was gathered around the Rector, who was in the midst of one of his stories. Although they could be lengthy, his tales were always very entertaining and every so often the group would erupt in hearty laughter. As Scrooge approached the gathering, Mrs. Langstone rose to join him. They no longer concerned themselves with the fact that others might notice their preference for each other's company.

Without realizing they had broken from the storytelling, Scrooge and Mrs. Langstone found themselves taking a turn about the ground floor, entertaining each other with bits of unimportant information and small private jokes. Eventually, they stopped under the arch near the entry hall. There was no particular reason to stop there, other than that neither had any wish to re-join the party, as yet. So, there they stood, comfortable in each other's presence. Scrooge happened to look up and discovered, dangling just above them, a goodly bunch of holly, cedar sprigs and mistletoe, tied with a bright red ribbon. They had unwittingly wandered under the kissing ball, but Mrs. Langstone was not yet aware of it.

Scrooge put one hand behind her back and pointed up. When she saw the ball she simply smiled, and remarked, "Oh, isn't that lovely. I hadn't noticed it. I wonder who made it.", but she gave no indication of moving on. His heart was racing, and he was beyond rational consideration. As a drowning man would seize a life buoy, he took hold of both her shoulders, turned her to face him and leaned down to impetuously kiss her — on the cheek. It was a safe thing to do, but it did not satisfy. She looked up and their eyes fastened on each other's, causing Scrooge to toss aside all sense of caution. He gently pulled her to him, bent toward her purposefully and pressed his lips to hers — not lightly, but with enough fervor to convey what both were feeling. They lingered in the kiss just a bit, lost in the intensity of the moment and the longed-for intimacy. They did not at all mind that they were close by the company of others who miraculously took no notice. God bless the Rector and his stories for that!

When they finally looked at each other again, Scrooge held Mrs. Langstone's hands in his and promptly forgot all of his practiced speeches, as well as the fears that had plagued him for months. Without realizing it for what it was, he took a leap of faith and spoke plainly, from his heart. He whispered simply, "Dearest Rebecca, have I a chance?"

Her smile made him somewhat light-headed. Then she whispered in return, "My Dear Ebenezer, it is not a matter of chance, for I have already settled on you." She quickly slipped her arm through his and together they wandered, a bit wobbly perhaps, back to the parlor, where they were only vaguely aware of all of the activity that surrounded them.

Christmas dinner was finally announced, and everyone took their places. Desiring to honor Scrooge as the elder of the family, Catherine placed him in her spot at the end of the table, opposite Fred. She would sit on Fred's right and Mrs. Langstone on Scrooge's right. Catherine did not concern herself with seating guests according to status, or in a way that would ensure good conversation, since it was another Symons rule that everyone at the table would converse with everyone else and that the talk should be always kindly, but lively.

There was much cause to rejoice at this table and Fred asked Scrooge if he would, as the patriarch, offer the blessing. Scrooge was pleased to do so since his heart was full near to bursting. The rector, who would normally have the responsibility of saying prayers, was pleased to nod his assent, and Scrooge did not hesitate. All heads bowed, and he began.

"Our blessed Father in Heaven, we have much for which to thank You. Each person here is a testament to Your faithfulness, and as we partake of this wonderful bounty that You have provided, we are mindful of the Baby in the manger — the One Who was born to save us, and in Whom we pray. We will gladly live with Christmas in our hearts all year long, and walk according to Your guidance, to the best of our abilities," and everyone said, "Amen!"

As with the seating arrangements and the rules regarding conversation, the Symons' Christmas dinner was also served in a style that was all their own. Following an excellent soup, a large platter of carved turkey was placed before Fred, to be portioned onto plates by him. The other dishes were relegated to a sideboard, to be offered by servants. The turkey and trimmings were prepared to perfection, and the guests well-matched, so dinner was a spirited success, with much of the conversation recalling the activities of the past several months.

During a lull that often shows itself at gatherings, Rector Gifford asked if anyone had received any happy surprises during the past twelve-month. Then he warned, "Fred's coming back to life cannot be claimed, since it was a happy surprise we all shared!"

Scrooge was first to respond. "I must shamefacedly admit that I was not aware of Mrs. Langstone's musical ability until she played the pianoforte at the Thornes' musicale." As soon as he made the remark he feared he had slighted Flora, the other pianist in the group, but quickly found that he had not. Flora clapped her hands together and cried, "Oh, yes, I heard about that!" She then addressed Mrs. Langstone directly by pleading, "I hope you may find time in future, to help me with my technique." Mrs. Langstone was delighted, and they agreed to set a date.

Lucy Carter admitted that she believed she had been struck by a thunderbolt when Mr. Carter appeared at her millinery shop after being in America for almost ten years. She said it certainly had been a happy surprise, but not immediately, since it had taken her a moment to decide who he was! Her fellow diners reacted with happy commotion, knowing what a joyous reunion it had turned out to be, in the end.

Rollo Norris bravely recalled that he had been surprised that the "spirited Mr. Scrooge" had managed to refrain from "having a go at the boaters, who were being so obstinate," and everyone jeered and clapped when Scrooge finished with, "Yes, I did, and I continued to stand stock still as Norris, here, attacked the man with his bare fists!"

Throughout dinner there was continued jovial banter and heartfelt remarks among the guests. Nearly halfway through the meal, between courses, Dick Wilkins stood, raised his glass and warmly announced, "Ladies and Gentlemen, just upstairs we have a beautiful new addition to the Symons family, and I know you will all join me in wishing Frederick Ebenezer Symons a long, happy and prosperous life — even into the Twentieth Century!" They all joyfully raised their glasses in agreement, while some pounded the table with their hands. After the rumpus had died down, Mrs. Sotherton wistfully remarked, "I wonder what sights he might see in that day!"

Several moments later Edwin Carter stood and raised his glass toward their host, saying, "I propose we do, together, formally salute the much heralded and very welcome return of our good friend, Fred Symons, back to life." The sentiment not only resulted in much agreement, but a few napkins were also employed to wipe away thankful tears. Mr. Carter did not mention the more grievous side of the adventure, out of respect for the half-brother who had not come back to life.

Fred himself rose to propose "a proper toast to congratulate and give best wishes to the new Mr. and Mrs. Carter." He insisted they were "the best example of long-lasting and joyful love" he had ever seen. Then he decided to include a toast to the entire brood of Cratchits who, although absent, "are so much an essential part of our lives, and stout friends, every one!" As he began to sit, one more thing occurred to him and he quickly returned to standing. He was thoroughly enjoying himself when he raised his glass and declared, "I also want to recognize the strength and accuracy of my sister-in-law, Flora, who is terribly effective at swinging an umbrella!" Everyone laughed heartily, and Flora blushed what Rollo Norris considered a very becoming shade of pink.

At last Scrooge stood and courageously raised his glass "to Mrs. Sotherton and her menagerie of odd acquaintances." There was a great deal of laughter and a resounding "hear-hear" when he added, "I only hope we may all be so fortunate and irrepressible as to someday be included on that extraordinary roster!"

After plum pudding and punch, as well as coffee for those who wished it, Mrs. Langstone and Flora each played several pieces on the pianoforte. Flora then accompanied the singing of Christmas carols before games were organized. It did not escape Scrooge's notice that Rollo Norris was particularly impressed with Flora's musical ability and, whenever possible, chose her as his partner during the games.

CS&O

Very late that night, while Scrooge snored in comfortable repose, Marley hovered near the bed. His appearance was unlike the spirit Scrooge was accustomed to seeing. He was not the apparition of a wasted life, nor was he bound by chains and money boxes. Instead, he emanated light. Although Scrooge did not hear him, Marley declared, "Well, old friend, you have come through two years as a 'regenerated' man. You have endured life's trials and soaked up its joys, and you have done well. Rest assured that I shall not go away, and you will have more years in which to experience life's up and downs, as well as countless blessings, both to give and to receive." With that he withdrew, but his departure was not his usual act of fading away. Instead, it was a quick explosion of intense brilliance, leaving a residue of supernatural warmth that permeated the entire room.

Made in the USA
Columbia, SC
04 March 2020